The King's
Arrow

The
King's
Arrow

Michael Cadnum

Viking

VIKING
Published by Penguin Group
Penguin Group (USA) Inc., 345 Hudson Street, New York, New York 10014, U.S.A.
Penguin Group (Canada), 90 Eglinton Avenue East, Suite 700, Toronto, Ontario, Canada M4P 2Y3
(a division of Pearson Penguin Canada Inc.)
Penguin Books Ltd, 80 Strand, London WC2R 0RL, England
Penguin Ireland, 25 St Stephen's Green, Dublin 2, Ireland (a division of Penguin Books Ltd)
Penguin Group (Australia), 250 Camberwell Road, Camberwell, Victoria 3124, Australia
(a division of Pearson Australia Group Pty Ltd)
Penguin Books India Pvt Ltd, 11 Community Centre, Panchsheel Park, New Delhi – 110 017, India
Penguin Group (NZ), 67 Apollo Drive, Rosedale, North Shore 0632, New Zealand
(a division of Pearson New Zealand Ltd)
Penguin Books (South Africa) (Pty) Ltd, 24 Sturdee Avenue, Rosebank, Johannesburg 2196, South Africa

Penguin Books Ltd, Registered Offices: 80 Strand, London WC2R 0RL, England

First published in the U.S.A. by Viking, a member of Penguin Group (USA) Inc., 2008

1 3 5 7 9 10 8 6 4 2

LIBRARY OF CONGRESS CATALOGING-IN-PUBLICATION DATA
Cadnum, Michael.
The king's arrow / Michael Cadnum. — 1st ed.
p. cm.
Summary: In England's New Forest on the second day of August, 1100, eighteen-year-old
Simon Foldre, delighted to be allowed to participate in a royal hunt as squire to the
Anglo-Norman nobleman Walter Tirel, finds his future irrevocably altered when,
during the hunt, he witnesses the possible murder of King William II.
ISBN 978-0-670-06331-4 (hardcover)
1. Tirel, Walter—Juvenile fiction. 2. William II, King of England, 1056?–1100—Assassination—Juvenile
fiction. [1. Tirel, Walter—Fiction. 2. William II, King of England, 1056?–1100—Assassination—Fiction.
3. Great Britain—History—William II, Rufus, 1087–1100—Fiction.
4. Coming of age—Fiction. 5. Middle Ages—Fiction.] I. Title.
PZ7.C11724Ki 2008
[Fic]—dc22
2007025313

Printed in U.S.A.
Set in Granjon
Book Design by Sam Kim

for Sherina

Blue water,
red bird—

I could never
forget to tell you

The King's Arrow

FOREWORD

HE NAME OF WALTER TIREL IS A PART OF the historical record, and the role he played in the violence suffered by King William II is also well established.

But mystery veils everything about the man. The events that led up to the fateful bow shot are likewise unknown. Nothing is recalled of Walter Tirel's possible motives for conspiring against the king—if that is what he did. Little is known of his escape, and even less is known about the man's character, or the nature of his associates—or of any particular friend who might have helped him.

This novel seeks to resolve one of the longest-standing mysteries in the English-speaking world. Did anyone accompany Walter Tirel on his desperate flight? Who helped him? What really happened in New Forest that day?

In this story many of the characters are fictional. But the hunt and the crisis that followed are real.

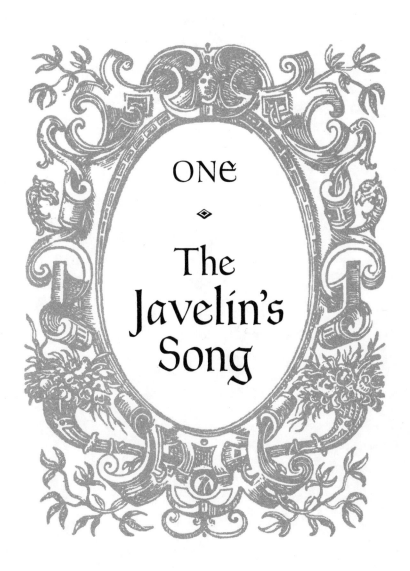

ONE

❖

The
Javelin's
Song

·1·

THE STALLION WAS AFRAID OF SHADOWS.

He danced sideways at the glimpse of a cloud sailing in a puddle, and tossed his mane at the sight of a grasshopper preening on a shaft of rye. His own silhouette spilling across the cart ruts made him snort and tear the road with his hooves, like an animal who wanted to fight something—anything—as soon as possible.

"Easy, Bel," said Simon, although the stallion gave no sign of knowing his own name.

There was real danger that Simon might fall off, despite the fact that he was supported from behind by the saddle's high cantle, and his feet were thrust into war stirrups. Bel took a deep, house-wide breath and held it, trying to loosen the saddle and dump Simon into the nearest puddle.

Simon hung on. The horse and all the leather trappings were for sale, if Simon could part with enough silver. The stallion would prove expensive, Simon feared, and he knew his mother could ill afford the price. Nonetheless, he thought, why not dream of owning such a steed for a few moments more?

The mount was indeed *bel*—handsome. Simon could scarcely wait to ride back down to the river and let Gilda admire the sight of Bel and his lucky rider—maybe this time she would be outdoors and looking up toward the road. But he did not want to risk ending up in the river muck, tossed aside by his ever-inventive steed, who by then would have come up with a way of rubbing his rider off against the mossy masonry of a wall, or knocking Simon's head off passing under Chad's Cross, the old stone monument on the way to the village.

Swein the horse breeder had been right to suggest that Simon take the steed for an afternoon's ride before he parted with precious metal. Now Bel was trying to take a chomp out of Blackfire, Certig's stalwart gelding, and out of the venerable servant himself, who exclaimed, "My lord Simon, look how he shows off his teeth!"

"Did he hurt you, Certig?" asked Simon, concern in his voice. The horse had about nine hundred teeth, he thought— far more than was required for chewing oats or biting servants.

Certig was Simon's manservant, and he had served Simon's father in the same capacity. He was adept at caring for animals—washing the horses' legs and mending buckles. In his earlier years he had been a sturdy companion and a good predictor of the weather.

"My lord," said Certig, rubbing his arm, "he did come close." Simon was concerned to see an expanding spot of blood on Certig's sleeve, but before he could inquire further, Bel gave a warning snort.

A far-off figure sprinted away from the leafy canopy of New Forest.

Even at this distance Simon recognized Edric.

Simon had known the hunter since boyhood—he had given Simon a fox's ear, for good luck. It was true that Edric was little better than a poacher, making his living by setting illegal snares in the king's forest. But he had a ready laugh and a pleasant singing voice, a delight to all who heard it.

Simon did not like the way Edric was running, like a man who had seen his own death. The cunning huntsman was running as hard as anyone could, tossing aside a handful of crossbow bolts to make his stride lighter.

Three horsemen broke from the verge of the woodland behind him. Prince Henry, King William Rufus's younger brother, was in the lead, urging, *"A coite, coite!"*—commanding his companions to spur their mounts.

Riding just behind the prince was Roland Montfort, the royal marshal, carrying a javelin, its iron point winking in the afternoon sun. The javelin was a spear with a leather loop attached to the shaft. The loop provided greater power to the throwing arm, but most men found the weapon hard to fling accurately from horseback.

Trailing behind was Oin the royal huntsman, riding like a man in no great hurry to overtake his quarry. Too far back, Simon believed, to restrain the marshal.

Edric fell to the ground far ahead of them, hidden by the windswept gorse. The horsemen did not see him for the moment, and they reined in their horses, struggling to control their mounts, pointing: *there, no—there*.

Edric crouched unseen to them under a flat, half-tilted stone, the fragment of some monument left by ancient folk, or—some believed—by supernatural beings still resident in the woods.

Stay, Simon warned him mentally, trying to send the message like a sling stone.

Edric, stay where you are.

He could call out to the prince—*Spare Edric, if you please, my lord prince*.

But the words froze in him. Simon had never spoken to the prince, and he had certainly never met King William, although on other summers he had watched from afar as the red-haired monarch rode back to his lodge, drunk in the saddle from a day hunting deer.

During the twelve years of his reign, the king and his brother nearly always visited New Forest during the fat season, the late summer weeks when the rutting roe deer were prime.

Despite its name, New Forest was as old as any other natural wild land. It got its designation from the fact that the old king, William the Conqueror, had claimed the place as his own within living memory, stripping the fields away from many of their traditional inhabitants. The forest, located along the coast in the extreme south of England, was dotted with a few long-established hamlets, but under law it was almost entirely given over to royal sport.

Simon had never dreamed of hunting in such a place. He was the son of a Norman officer and an English noblewoman. To a Norman man-at-arms Simon looked every inch the Englishman, while to a local shepherd he resembled a foreign lord. It was true that both king's men and field hands always spared him a smile and a kind word. But Simon faced a future of divided happiness, knowing too much of both English umbrage and Norman self-importance to feel at home in either camp.

Now Edric broke from his cover, and began to run again.

Saddle girths creaked, and snaffle bits jingled, the horse furnishings giving out rhythmic complaints as the riders closed in on the fugitive.

Simon called, "Flee, Edric, like a buck hare!"

Edric did as he was told, sprinting with a will, but right in the direction of Simon and his retainer. As the poacher reached the crest of the field, so close Simon could see the sweat on his face, Bel decided to play a role in events.

The steed did not plunge or fight the reins or shy—shy and stay where he was as many a horse would have done. Perhaps the roan took a particular offense at the sight of Edric's fowling weapon, the crossbow beating a steady rhythm at the hunter's side, or at his tattered sleeves, streaming behind as the poacher flew. Or perhaps the horse was a creature of such spirit that he could take one glance at the fugitive and decide he did not like the angle of the freedman's cap.

Simon was powerless to stop him. The stallion hurried to meet the approaching runner and lunged. He flattened his ears and attacked, snapping the air by Edric, and snapping again, and getting a good mouthful of the yeoman's shoulder.

Edric fell.

The horse had hurt Edric. As he struggled to his feet, Bel shifted his heavy hooves and blocked Edric's escape, even as he presented Simon to the possibility of danger.

The royal marshal powered his javelin high into the air as Simon tugged at the reins, moving to block Certig from danger, and putting his own body in the likely path of the spear.

· 2 ·

THE JAVELIN HUMMED, A SURPRISINGLY LOW sound, like the approach of a large moth.

The weapon descended with a gathering speed, its sound increasingly high-pitched—and shockingly close to Simon. When it lanced home the projectile was—at that last instant—invisible. And then suddenly it was all too visible once again, the wooden shaft erupting from the back of a struggling mortal like a long, wooden extension of the poacher's backbone.

Edric reached out for a support that was not there—a staff, perhaps, or the arm of a vanished friend. He reached to cling to Bel's bridle and missed. He fell to the ground. Simon knew that the injury was grievous, but wanted to believe that shock and suddenness would render Edric insensible to the pain.

"Quiet yourself, dear Edric," exclaimed Simon, reaching down from his saddle to grasp the jutting shaft.

His gloved hand reached—but he could not bring himself to seize the shaft, thinking that the effort would only stir more agony in the man. The poacher hitched himself nearly double, trying to turn around, struggling to work his body inside out as Prince Henry approached.

Edric managed a final laugh—a bloody, ragged gash of a smile—as though the cruel joke was not lost on him: the poacher pinched.

Simon had once seen a woodcutter bleed to death from an accidental wound, and he had seen neighboring farmers sicken and fade despite the prayers of family and friends. But he had never seen a man die at the hands of another, certainly not as Edric was dying, the prince probing and stabbing with the weapon as the poor soul lay bleeding within the shadows of the horsemen.

Simon breathed a prayer to Heaven for the broken-bodied, now silent Edric. The man expired in the blood-soaked earth, his sins unconfessed, and Simon felt the coming sorrow of Edric's wife and children in their ramshackle homestead. He could not bring himself to look at the prince, let alone the marshal.

"My lord prince," Simon began, when he could make a sound. He was going to add a word of welcome—stiff and unfelt courtesy, but necessary all the same. *Could you not have given him a lash or two, and sent him home?*

His death was legal, Simon knew. Poaching the king's game was a capital crime, and the king had commanded swift punishment to such criminals. But still—Simon remembered Edric's chuckle, and the way he danced on market day, quick-footed in work and play.

Simon would have asked, *Why, my lord prince, did you have to kill him?*

But Prince Henry himself wore a sad smile. "I thank you, friend, whoever you are," said the prince. "You did well to block his escape—although it is a shame to see a man die so."

The royal huntsman arrived at last. Oin fitzBigot had allowed Simon to ride in the New Forest since boyhood, if not to actually hunt there. "My lord prince," said Oin, "this is Simon Foldre."

"Who?" asked the prince absently.

"My lord," said Oin, "I told you he'd make a good hunting companion to the king's friend Walter Tirel from Picardy."

Simon's heart leaped at the sound of the well-known noble name. And at the promise of a royal hunt—that sort of honor had always been beyond the reach of Simon and his widowed mother. No one but the king and his favorites could legally so much as bend a bow in New Forest.

The royal marshal was silent, eyeing the shadowy oaks beyond the grazing land. Like the king, the marshal was a red-haired man with blue eyes, and a fighting man's thick neck and deep chest. Roland was in charge of the king's personal security, and he protected the gateways, halls, larder, and kennels of the king with his personal attention and the well-honed talents of his staff. In the absence of the prince, Simon would have hazarded his future in a confrontation with Roland right then.

From within the woods now came a series of shrills on a horn, answered by a distant series of similar blasts from near the river, a woodsman's code.

Roland said, "Already word of this poacher's death is spreading, all the way to the salt shore. Let them all respect King William's property."

Simon was impressed at the marshal's ability to interpret the horn blowers' code, but not surprised. It was said, half in jest, that Roland met with spiders every night, collecting information on everything from cowpox to taxes.

There were lingering figures on the forest verge, no doubt apprentice poachers, stunned at the fate of their master. No human beings actually lived in the woods, although there were tales of half-mad felons who had escaped the law for so many years they had grown cloven hooves and horns.

The shadowy observers ran off. Only one lingered at the edge of the sunlight, one of Edric's nephews, unless Simon was mistaken, waiting until he could safely steal forth and claim his uncle's body.

Not three months earlier Simon had come upon Roland wrestling a goose girl to the ground near the bridgehead. Simon had heard a gasping plea for help, parted the saplings, heard the young woman's grateful thanks, and found himself eye to eye with Roland as the young woman escaped.

"He's the sole son of your father's loyal swordsman Fulcher Foldre," Oin was saying. "Fulcher married an English beauty, a duke's daughter."

"Is that right?" inquired Henry. He was dark-haired and had dark eyes, and usually spoke quietly. His cloak bore a silver-and-jet pin shaped like a falcon or a griffin, or some other beaked creature. This single ornament, Simon guessed, was worth more than all the plates, pitchers, swords, and charms of a noble English household.

"My lord prince, my mother's father," Simon said, "was Usher of Aldham."

"Oh, yes?" said Prince Henry with mildest interest, melancholy, it seemed, at participating in the death of the poacher.

"And Usher's family," Simon continued, "called these fields home since Noah's flood."

Roland reached down and seized the projecting shaft of the javelin. He withdrew the weapon from Edric's body with a twist. "This dead felon, Simon," said the marshal, "could make a similar claim, along with many a marsh leech in England."

Simon was speechless at this insult. He was not fully armed, but he was far from defenseless. Men out riding for hunting or sport usually carried a stabbing sword. Simon had a formidable blade at his belt, with which his father had once frightened off a party of drunken English squires.

Simon's hand went to the hilt of this weapon.

· 3 ·

IT WAS THE YEAR OF OUR LORD 1100.

Nearly thirty-five years had passed since William the Conqueror had sailed from Normandy, the countryside across the Channel from England. He had arrived with knights and squires, and destroyed King Harold's army. Norman noblemen had replaced the English-speaking aristocracy throughout the realm. The best land had been confiscated from English families and given out as rewards to the victor's loyalists.

There had been bitter resentment among the suddenly powerless natives, and towns to the north had rebelled until King William had devastated farmsteads and villages, causing the deaths of untold numbers. Now the Conqueror's son, William Rufus—the Red—continued the mastery of the defeated kingdom, ensuring that his friends and cousins held positions of power.

Wherever William Rufus traveled, his men stole what they fancied, destroyed what they chose, and even the most distinguished English families were powerless to protest. The current king was thought to be a worthy heir to the throne, but where the first King William had crushed his enemies with a dashing ruthlessness, the current king was thought to be ruthless without much originality. To his father's passion for the hunt, William Rufus added a zeal for the stag and hound that was already legendary.

The eighteen summers of Simon's life had seen some gradual political and social changes. While no Norman in a position of power ever bothered to learn much English, every Englishman of ambition studied the language of the conquerors. More than a few Norman aristocrats fell in love with local women and married them, and some English noblemen were lately being awarded minor positions of stewardship. It could be easily argued that Norman rule was not so different, summer and winter, from the English feudal establishment.

Now Simon was absorbing Roland's insult, as Prince Henry was giving a wave of his hand, reassuring Simon. "For myself, I would rather this lively poacher were still alive. But my brother is king, and his command is law."

"God keep him," offered the marshal.

The prince gave Simon a searching, but friendly, glance.

"Walter Tirel," the prince said, "was mentioning over morning wine today that he wanted to hunt with an English *varlet* who knows the woods."

A hunting varlet would be expected to act as the game servant—to carry the quiver, hand out the arrows as needed, and have an eye for the woods and its creatures. To serve a nobleman at the royal hunt, even in a secondary role, was a magnificent privilege.

Roland leaned from his saddle and spat into the grass.

Bad feeling existed between Roland and Walter Tirel, as everyone knew, going back generations. One of the marshal's forebears had quarreled with Walter's ancestor, an earlier duke of Poix, on the summit of a bridge, and the duke's horse had trod upon the marshal's ancestor, or soiled him—the songs about it were amusing and varied. Helping Walter could only irritate Roland, and this further pricked Simon's ambition.

Besides, Walter was widely regarded on both sides of the Channel as a wealthy nobleman, with a lively spirit and—rumor had it—a beautiful, virtuous younger sister who was as yet unmarried. Walter would make a powerful acquaintance, if only Simon would allow such a soaring ambition to enter his mind.

"My lord prince," said Simon, "I will serve the king and his guest with all my honor."

"We can't," said Marshal Roland, looking right at Simon, "let the Count of Poix step into the woods with one of our two-legged English dogs."

Prince Henry turned and gave the marshal a silencing glance. Insulting the English nobility was considered dull-witted sport and bad manners, although to Simon's knowledge it was a common practice. Prince Henry was considered more gentle in spirit than his father had been, and more understanding than his brother the king. More than one Englishman had whispered over beer that Henry would make a better sovereign by far than his red-haired, red-handed sibling.

The prince turned again to Simon and gave him a pleasant smile. "No, we can't, really, let the nobleman walk about with some English toadstool who can't tell *main* from *maine*. But you do speak well enough, Simon or Lymon, whoever you are—grandson of your grandfather."

"My lord prince," interjected Roland, "this young man should be cautioned that if the least harm comes to Walter Tirel, it will cost him his head."

Hunting was a dangerous enterprise, and many noblemen had died of hunting accidents over the years, partly caused by drunkenness, and partly because the greenwood-hued cloaks hunters wore to hide from the deer made them easy to mistake for game. Such fatal accidents often resulted in further violence, as the friends of the stricken hunter set upon the perpetrator, however innocent his blunder might have been, and cut him to pieces.

But the prince was no longer interested in the conversation. "This stallion is two years old, perhaps?" inquired Henry, reaching for Bel's bridle.

The horse nosed the prince's hand, shifted its head to one side to give the royal brother a glance, and took a long, four-legged pace back, disregarding Simon's whispered, "Be still!"

"Little older than that, my lord prince," said Simon. "He's as spirited as the westward sea."

"I'll take him," said the prince.

Simon started, and glanced about. Surely he misunderstood.

Oin's expression was pained, one eye shut, as though against bitter wind. Anger swept upward, through Simon's spleen, the organ of ire, radiating heat down through his limbs.

"Hurry, hurry," exclaimed the prince impatiently. "This is an English habit, is it not, to gape around with their mouths open? Dismount, my good Simon. My brother was in an ill humor all this week, and such a gift will brighten his mood. You will walk home."

Simon did not dismount. He clung to the high pommel of the saddle. Bel's leather furnishings alone were worth a servant's annual wages, expensive tack Swein had loaned Simon with a gracious laugh. Losing the horse—having the stallion stolen by the prince—would be a painful shame to Simon, and a stern financial challenge he would have to make good to Swein and his family.

"Look," said the prince, "how eager Bel is to have a new master. This will be a gift for my brother, to ease his spirits when he learns that there are poachers in his woods."

The prince was cordial enough to smile as he spoke, but it was a royal smile, welcoming and dismissive at once. "This gift will help to ensure the king's permission," the prince added, "that you may hunt with us tomorrow."

· 4 ·

OW, SIMON WONDERED, WAS HE GOING TO explain all this to his mother?

He nearly asked the question out loud, but it was the sort of question one did not put to a servant, even a trusted old hand like Certig. Besides, the venerable servant had suffered a serious injury the past autumn when a branch broke from a tree during a storm and struck him on the head. Certig had been unconscious for a day and a night, and ever since Simon had not wanted to cause the man any more worry than necessary.

"Do you suppose, my lord," asked Certig, "that misfortune might someday seize Marshal Roland?"

There was one smarting sword prick on Simon's forearm. Roland had smiled as he had thrust the blade, not with happiness so much as quiet concentration, as a leatherworker might, punching a neat hole with an awl. Simon had not made a sound. The prince had protested, "Leave off, Marshal Roland!" and Roland had shrugged and sheathed his weapon.

The little wound smarted.

Influences, uncanny but powerful, were known to shape events. Stars and planets, imps and devils, all worked on a person's life. Simon recognized that this particular mildly sunny day—the first of August, the Feast of Saint Peter in Chains—was for him personally a period of unparalleled bad luck. In truth, it was hard to imagine a day of sharper misfortune.

Simon headed home on Blackfire—a sweet-natured mount but a plodder—as Certig walked along with a hazel switch. The servant was too kindhearted to use it on the horse, but he let the flicking shadow of the hazel rod remind the creature not to stop and crop the summer grass along the road.

Simon had protested, but Certig had insisted that no serving man of character would let his lord walk while the servant rode. As for Simon, perched in the worn and peeling saddle, he did not bother kicking the horse or urging the animal into a canter. What was the use? It was no pleasure for Simon to pass gleaners raking the last of the hay and cowherds enjoying the shade of trees, all of whom had seen him earlier that day riding in high fashion.

"Good afternoon, Simon," they called, each one of them,

even the most taciturn oxherd, who rarely spoke.

Simon smiled and waved, wishing that he were invisible.

The river twinkled through the hawthorns, the rising tide soothing upward through the water-rounded stones. The Normans called the river Beau Lieu—"beautiful place"—while the English traditionally referred to it as The Water, as though the power to grace the land with vibrant names had long ago failed them.

A ship careened at the end of a long, yellow rope. This was the *Saint Bride*, the strong-timbered vessel owned by Gilda and her brother and used for trade across the Channel, where wheels of New Forest cheese were exchanged for Low Countries linen.

Like most seagoing vessels, the ship owed much of her design to the Norse fighting ships and freighters of great fame. While there were many other ships along the riverbank, and a burgeoning industry of shipwrights near the river's mouth, few of the local craft were as seaworthy nor, thought Simon, as pleasing to the eye.

And none were named after such a popular saint. Saint Bride—or Bridget, as she was also known—was during her lifetime responsible for an impressive miracle: On the arrival of unexpected guests, travelers from afar, she transformed gray dishwater into sparkling new ale. Her visitors rejoiced, and were refreshed. As a result, she had become over the years a saint associated with bounty of every sort, and Gilda and her brother had thrived under her care.

Simon had hoped to cut a fine figure on his new steed, but now he hoped the shadows of the trees would hide them as they clopped methodically along the road. The nick in his left arm was not bleeding anymore, and a little vinegar would cleanse the trifling wound.

But his delayed, as yet unspoken response to Certig's query would have been *no*.

No, Roland would not be struck down by man or Heaven anytime soon. He was a king's man, with a family back in Montfort, a wealthy Norman village Simon, who had never been across the Channel, could only imagine. He pictured happy piglets and lambs and beaming farming folk, proud that one of their lords had been raised in London and was now serving the king of England.

Simon supposed, with a grim whimsy, that if Roland dined on the infants of English peasantry—actually ate them for midday meal—he would be scolded by some royal steward for his choice of food, but suffer no special punishment.

"Isn't that Gilda," Certig was asking, "down by the sternpost?"

"Hush, Certig."

"Surely it is."

Let us steal past, dear Certig, Simon wanted to say, *and escape any notice.*

But it was too late.

The individual beside the ship looked up, and was not fair-haired Gilda at all but her brother Oswulf, who resembled his sister the way a blade resembled a feather. Tuda was with him, the strong-armed helper dragging a coil of mooring cable up to the boathouse. Tuda rarely offered an opinion on anything, and Simon liked him for his cheerful silence. Tuda's grandfather had built a henhouse on stilts, a local landmark, proof against weasels.

"What are the horns telling us, Simon?" called Oswulf. A river man was not entirely familiar with the horn blasts and calls used by poachers and other freebooting yeomen, but it was also possible that Oswulf knew full well what was being said.

"Oh, Oswulf, it is dreadful," said Certig. "A terrible thing, impossible to talk about."

Like everyone Simon knew, Certig did not want to say plainly what evil had taken place. To put words to misfortune made it worse, and confirmed it beyond hope.

Oswulf approached as Blackfire teased green acorns from the overhead branches. "Lord Simon, what has happened?" Oswulf asked. Although he and his sister were not of noble birth, their family had lived along the watercourse for as long as anyone could recall, and their family name was, by common usage, Shipman—*Scipmann*.

Edric had been well liked, but at the same time the scamp

had been no one's idea of a saint. Simon resented having to enunciate the news. "The lord marshal's javelin," he said, "has found our old friend Edric."

"But only wounded him?" asked Oswulf hopefully.

"Oh, worse than wounded, Oswulf," said Certig. "Far, far worse."

"You saw it happen?" gasped Oswulf.

"We were right there," exclaimed Certig, to Simon's discomfiture. "He died in our very shadows!"

"And what, Simon," asked Oswulf, narrowing his eyes, "did you do to defend our friend?"

If only I could see Gilda, thought Simon. Surely that fairminded young woman would understand. Simon shook his head, indicating that he had been helpless to defend Edric. Someday, Simon vowed silently to himself, he would strike the marshal down.

"Please give my greetings to your sister," Simon managed to say.

Oswulf turned away, too troubled to speak.

Just before Simon reached home, there was a slight rise in the road, the point where, it was said, a giant had been buried by the legendary hero Tom of Sway. Some said the giant merely enjoyed a slumber long and deep and would awaken, cheerful but famished after his long nap.

From Giant's Crest, Simon could see his home. Aldham

Manor, the house where he and his mother lived, had been built many years ago by Simon's grandfather, and it had replaced a centuries-old dwelling. The manor's lime-washed walls were beautiful in the afternoon sunlight.

It was unmistakably simply what it was: a thriving but unadorned location surrounded by farm and pasture. It was unpretentious, practical, and all the more lovely, in Simon's eyes, for all that. Far beyond the rambling manor house, on a hill, was the much newer tower built by Simon's father.

The structure was a keep of flint and mortar, a rugged redoubt made to withstand siege. Simon admired the tower, and enjoyed the fresh smell of it, and the practical way the family and servants could pull up the drawbridge and be safe from attack. No enemy had ever clattered up the road, and his mother had never walked the distance up the hill to visit the keep, not in ten years.

But she made sure, when the account scrolls were studied at the end of every harvest, that silver was set aside for the well rope and new shutter latches, where they were needed, with enough to provide crossbow bolts and slings. When Simon asked her why she bothered to maintain Foldre Castle, she would say that bloody-taloned war could swoop from any sky.

This was the difficulty, Simon knew, with his mother. She loved laughter, shared the richly flavored Aldham manor ale with the poor, and clapped her hands in time to the minstrel's capers, but she required more. The daughter of a warrior of noble name, the widow of one of the Conqueror's favorites, she hungered for a respected station in a kingdom that valued English ladies but little.

"Do you think Walter Tirel of Poix will turn out to be any better than the others?" Simon was asking now.

"I've heard that Walter Tirel is a man with a sharp sword, my lord," said Certig. "But a man of grace, I've been told."

"Who says this?"

"A plate servant can tell you a man's character better than his priest, and such word travels across the Channel. We don't see a man of Walter's Tirel's renown," added Certig, "in our woodland very often."

Walter Tirel. The name had a fine sound to it, Simon thought—a definite music.

An oxcart teetered and swayed its course up the deeply rutted way, conveying a lopsided load of milled oats, piled so high the load was sure to tumble.

Plegmund had worked the land of Simon's ancestors, planting grain and breeding goats. He was a peasant of substance, one of Simon's most prosperous tenants, and he had recently purchased an iron candle-prick—an iron bullock with a spike on its head for a candle—a fine object crafted in Portsmouth and admired by his neighbors. Simon had paid a visit, to admire the handiwork.

"My lord Simon," said Plegmund, "there's no need to worry about old Plegmund. My team will make it over the ridge easy as a song." He put a hand to his mouth in a caricature of conspiracy. "We must be quick and quiet. I hear the king's guard are about, making sure all is calm."

Calm was meant ironically. The king's men had a notorious intolerance for boredom, and London and her environs had been set alight in recent years and nearly destroyed by armed men with time on their hands.

"I do believe, Plegmund," said Simon, "that you will need our help."

The ancient flax-cloth sacks were packed to the point of bursting through their oft-mended seams. Blackfire tossed his head at the smell of so much fresh horse feed seeping through the cloth.

The recent arrival of the royal court—with its dozens of cupbearers, clerks, and armorers—drove up prices and made such grain all the more scarce. Plegmund had made an enormous purchase and would no doubt resell the oats to the king's stables, with Simon and his mother keeping a good share of the profits.

"I might need, perhaps, a small amount of help, my lord," said Plegmund. "Just this once."

The cart's wheels had never been perfectly round, having been made from the trunk of a great oak cut long ago into slices. Wear had shaped them into obstinate oblongs, and

Simon marveled that the team of oxen could travel from ford to farm with such a wobbling, unsteady wagon. It was true that Plegmund's oxen were the stuff of myth—massive brutes, with dewlaps that hung nearly to the road.

Simon shoved so hard the yoke shifted forward on the oxen, and the big animals took a few uncharacteristic light steps, nearly trotting, relieved at the quickening of their load. Nonetheless, the rise was too steep for the ambitious burden, and the cart groaned to a stubborn halt.

They heaved with all their strength against the cart.

The greeting of a young woman made them interrupt their efforts.

· 5 ·

"I WOULDN'T CARRY SUCH A LOAD FOR YOU, Simon," said the young woman as she hurried up the road.

"Not for Simon," said Plegmund, "but maybe for some other lucky man under Heaven."

"Oswulf said you stopped by," said Gilda, "but would not linger to talk with me."

"What else did he tell you?" asked Simon.

"My brother was in a strange temper." She took Simon by the hand and led him to the tall hedge beside the road.

"Meet me tonight, Gilda," said Simon, "under the big chestnut."

"Tonight?" asked Gilda coyly. "This very night I believe our cat is due—she'll have six kittens or I'm a mule."

"Please," said Simon.

"Whatever is wrong with Oswulf, after all?" she asked, as Simon continued to hold on to both of her hands. "He says he'll never bear the sight of you again, but he will say nothing of why."

Oswulf was given to quickly changing moods, and often made sweeping statements he would later forget. For his part, Simon did not want to put the day's events into words at all. He found the effort painful as he said, with as much elegant simplicity as he could muster, "The royal marshal has acted, with fatal results."

"Roland Montfort?"

Simon nodded.

"What has he done?"

"Roland has killed Edric."

Gilda released his hands.

"Stuck him through with a javelin throw," added Simon, hating the words as he spoke them. *You see,* he chided himself, *how much better it is to keep quiet?*

"Edric," she said at last, "was going to bring me a woodcock."

"No other man but Roland," said Simon in a tone of matter-of-fact despair, "could have killed anyone at such a distance."

She weighed the implication of this statement.

"You were there, were you, Simon?"

Simon's shame was personal, in that he had not fought for

Edric's life, and made worse by the implication that as a half-Norman scion he might approve of such butchery. Simon was fully aware that he and Gilda were speaking in English, the language of hill and river, but not the language of government.

Simon kept his answer short. "I was."

She made no farewell, no promise to see him that night. She was there one moment, and gone the next.

Her sudden absence struck Simon as further proof that the day was being warped out of true by some errant star or planet.

"I've penned my goats and placed a double watch all night, both of my sons," said Plegmund. The robust peasant had the merciful sense to speak softly, of a gently distracting subject.

"Goats?" Simon asked, only half aware what was being discussed.

"I've penned them up." Goats were thought to spoil a woodland—deer did not like to browse where goats had been grazing. "Grestain, the marshal's sergeant, said he'd kill every last kid," added Plegmund, "if I didn't look to them."

Plegmund said this not in a tone of complaint, but as a workingman talking about a force of nature, relentless and age-old. There was, however, a weary, cordial challenge to his remark. Simon was reminded how potentially violent the royal spearmen were, and how powerless a half-bred Norman lord would ever prove to be.

"How is Caesar?" asked Simon.

"Oh, old Caesar's been eating nettles, my lord," said Plegmund with a laugh, "and kills everything he pisses on."

Caesar was the prolific and fierce billy of Plegmund's herd, gray and powerful, although blind in one eye from chasing a well-armed Norman squire several summers ago.

"We could use an English king like that," said Certig.

It was one of those blunt remarks Certig came out with sometimes—all the more since his injury. And it could be considered treason, punishable by death.

As though to underscore the danger of such talk, a knot of horsemen appeared, four of them, cantering easily up the road, Grestain the marshal's sergeant foremost, clad in the blue-and-gold livery of the royal court.

"Hurry," urged Simon, "get this cart up and over the hump."

It was the way of the marshal's men to try to join in with such tasks, helping to push carts or rescue cats, so that the local people might feel more friendly and inadvertently blurt a word of disrespect against the king. Such armed men had been known to help themselves to local produce, and even someone of Simon's good name would be hard-pressed to quell a band of greedy guardsmen.

They were too late. Grestain called out a greeting, and common good manners required an exchange of pleasantries.

"You have overloaded your cart," added the marshal's

man, speaking heavily accented English. The oxen turned their yoked heads toward the snorts and sneezes of the horses. One of the bovine behemoths shook his head, whether in dull fellowship or because a fly teased his eyes, it was hard to tell. The yoke shifted back and forth, and the cart creaked.

"Oh, yes, indeed I have, my lord sergeant," agreed Plegmund.

"I might almost wonder, my lord," said Grestain, turning his attention to Simon, "if your folk are shipping weapons under their oats." The sergeant had a broad, weathered face, and a solid-looking body, like a man who had been put together by a saddle maker, and constructed to last a long time.

Simon knew all the marshal's men by sight and reputation. For years they had ruined stiles, defiled wells, and set animals alight in the name of amusement. Repairing the damage they had caused over the seasons was a chief burden on the manor's earnings.

"Ha-ha," exclaimed Plegmund, his forced laughter sounding nothing like the real thing.

Simon said evenly, "My people are loyal subjects, Sergeant."

His tone was deliberately and coolly dismissive, and Grestain was quick to say, "Of course, my lord."

Grestain was a sandy-haired man, with sun-browned features and yellow eyes. Simon knew him to be Roland's aide, a West Country man trying to rise in a world of knights who preferred dull imported wine to the local cider.

"I herded oxen," the sergeant said, "when I was a boy. I have never been happier."

"The ox," said Simon, judiciously, "is an agreeable beast."

When a lawman spoke, he was collecting information. Even the lord of a manor had to speak with care. Oxen certainly seemed like a safe subject, in Simon's view, and subject to no controversy, but Plegmund's nearside ox was a brute of spirit, and had once swung its massive head at a traveling flute player.

Grestain and two of the sergeant's men dismounted and heaved their weight against the cart, and together with the others they powered the load over what had to be a very large slumbering giant. This, too, was typical of the king's men, thought Simon. An imperious bunch, they often wanted simply to be liked.

Only afterward—with farewells given and taken, and best wishes for a pleasant afternoon—did Plegmund confide to Simon in a whisper, "I have an ax under my load, if they'd searched."

"One ax is not a rebellion, Plegmund," said Simon with a smile. He was glad Grestain and his gang had ridden off, and he was eager to be home.

"And I have that sword I bought from the Bremen town squire," added Plegmund. "And that spear I found out by the old wellhead and mended myself last winter. And one or two other blades I keep by me, you might say, against danger."

"Danger, dear Plegmund," said Simon uneasily, "is exactly what you will discover."

"But I hear of trouble everywhere," said Plegmund. "Coming trouble, my lord, and all of us unready."

· 6 ·

SIMON WAS GLAD TO BE HOME AGAIN, under the smoke-cured oak timbers of the manor house.

"I must pay Swein at once, as soon as I give him the tidings," said Simon. "The horse breeder has a temper, and we don't want him riding off to try to wrest Bel out of the royal stable."

"Ah, Simon, Swein will endure this indignity, and so will you," said his mother with an air of indisputable judgment. "I shall pay a visit to Edith," she added, thinking of Edric's widow, "and her two daughters."

Simon stood in the wide, quiet hall of his family home. His sword nick had been bandaged with clean linen, and after a bite of wine-soaked simnel bread, he was not feeling the least fatigue or pain. Or only a very little.

His mother—Widow Christina, as she was known—was beyond finding any bad news shocking. Her husband, a knight who had, as the story went, once staved off a mad dog from King William's camp, had died of a fall from his horse in midsummer, ten years before.

He had been a seasoned campaigner when he took Christina's hand in marriage. He had brought over a Norman wife and daughter only to lose them to black fever, and Simon had more than once heard his father tell Christina that she was his *enseignier*—evidence of his blessing, and his second, undeserved chance at happiness.

Christina had survived her bereavement, and learned to laugh again and enjoy the sound of her son singing poems beside the fire, but a quality of sorrow was always with her. Simon knew that her dreams of personal vindication included Simon's marriage to a Norman family of wealth, if only to prove that her family had the equal of any pedigree, on either side of the Channel.

"You will pay Swein this silver, Simon," said Christina, returning from a cupboard. "And tell him we join him in praying for God's help against royal criminals."

This was the last cut-treasure from the family strongbox, and there was no way of knowing how long this silver fragment had been stored, wrapped in fine-spun cloth to keep it from tarnishing. Some tankard or arm ring from the just-past age, when the Vikings raided the English coasts, must have yielded this precious metal, some Norwegian's battle hoard.

Usher of Aldham had been a tireless defender against the Norse.

Aldham estate currently prospered, but the mending of walls, relining of wells, and repair and breeding and replanting all took a toll. Christina and Simon were land-wealthy without having much ready money.

"What do you think of Prince Henry, Simon?" his mother was asking. "I have never laid eyes on the man."

"Prince Henry has some great subject on his mind," Simon said. "I doubt even Bel's high spirits will give him much happiness."

"Henry wishes he were king, I have heard," said Christina. "The middle brother Robert is in Jerusalem on crusade, and King William the eldest drinks and ruts his way back and forth across our kingdom. I hear that Henry's pigeon hawk hatched a two-headed chick."

Simon had to laugh at this. "That's a sure sign, Mother— but of what?"

Christina laughed quietly in turn. "I confess I'm not entirely certain—but when is an omen as straightforward as a beggar's curse?"

The sound of riders in the dooryard silenced them.

Simon counted the hooves by sound—three mounts, at least, along with the *chin-chink* of chain mail and the rasp of a spear butt dragged along the ground.

The house servants gathered outside, English and Norman

speech too tangled for Simon to make out. There was no need to fear—Aldham's housemen could stave off a good-sized army, and had done just that during Viking times. Certig's voice could be heard above all, the retainer mastering not a word of Norman speech but calling out in English, "Tell your lord, my good herald, that his horse has squashed our rooster!"

Simon strode to the wall and took down his father's sword, a blade with a red carnelian jewel in its hilt. He and Oin had practiced fighting with broadswords and two-handed swords, too, and while Simon had never actually struck steel in earnest, he was not going to embarrass himself.

Alcuin, the chief house servant, hurried into the smoky firelight and said, "My lady, a noble visitor asks to speak with Simon."

"Who disturbs our peace, Alcuin?" asked Christina with an air of hopefulness. She received few guests of note, and while she was gracious to scullery servant and abbot alike, she was habitually eager to be pleasantly surprised by a day's events, and routinely slightly disappointed.

"A Norman nobleman," said the houseman. He said this in the manner of *Need I say more?*

Alcuin had attended Simon's father as a plate servant, pouring wine from a ewer in the days of Simon's boyhood, when coin was more plentiful. Alcuin had grown gray as his duties increased. "He is of a name unfamiliar to me, if it please my lady," he added. "And Certig is sore upset. Sangster the breed cock has been stepped on by a horse."

"Is the poor bird badly injured?" asked Christina.

Sangster was the fire and spirit of the dooryard, a menace to man and beast, and a local legend. The chicks he sired proved fertile and healthy, and the red-feathered warrior would not be easily replaced.

"Worse than hurt, I fear, my lady," said Alcuin.

He was his mistress's loyal chief of staff, and he knew how she liked to learn all she could in the way of detailed gossip. "This noble fellow wears a red agate ring and a cap with a rich plume, my lady," he offered. "His herald says that he is one Walter Tirel, of a place called Po-icks."

"He is Count of Poix," prompted Simon, with a sensation of expectant pride. He was thrilled inwardly, sure that Walter would live up to his reputation. "Walter Tirel is the king's guest, and I hunt with him tomorrow, as Heaven wills it."

"Oh, Simon," breathed Christina, "I would so enjoy meeting this visitor!"

Alcuin waited expectantly, something unsaid in his eyes— a caution, perhaps.

The chief servant took his instructions from the lady of the house but, as was customary, even a widowed mother deferred to the wishes of the eldest male in her family.

For a moment Simon's pride allowed him to think that the illustrious nobleman had ridden out of his way to meet his prospective companion. Perhaps this Walter of Poix was so good-hearted—and Oin fitzBigot so generous in his descriptions of Simon's knowledge of the woodland—that the Norman lord had decided that he had to meet this son of Fulcher Foldre at once.

This hope was soon shattered.

· 7 ·

VOICES IN THE DOORYARD HAD BEEN GETTING louder.

Now the wooden barrier to the outside burst open.

Late-afternoon sunlight poured through the lingering cooking smoke of the chamber as a mantled, tall man strode into the interior. He was accompanied by a guard who wore a broad, black-buckled belt and cross-gartered boots, and a youthful herald, who pressed his cap onto his head to keep it in place, and took quick steps to keep up with his older companions.

The herald, Simon thought, could have been ten or twelve years of age, with blond hair and the emblem of his office—a document case adorned with fine stones—suspended by a chain around his neck. He wore a knife at his hip.

"My lord," said Christina, "I am pleased to welcome you to our home." She spoke the Norman dialect with an English burr—a beautiful accent to Simon's ears.

Walter Tirel's appearance did not disappoint Simon in the least. He had brown eyes and a short, neat, golden-colored beard. His mantle was long, with its hood thrown back, and was made of lambs' wool dyed deep blue or green—it was hard to tell in this interior light. Like most noblemen, he looked and acted like a man ready to kill someone—not angry so much as ready for whatever came. His presence did not necessarily threaten immediate murder, Simon knew. It was a fashion among noblemen to seem dangerous.

How fine, thought Simon, it would be to have such an ally!

Their Norman visitor bowed briefly before Christina, and said that he was honored, all prettily enough, but with a quality of haste that was hardly the best form.

He faced Simon at once for the more immediate business. He was almost as tall and strongly built as Simon, who was no stripling.

"Where are you keeping your horses?" demanded the nobleman.

The statement might have sounded forcefully jovial, except for the tone, which was one of pure insistence.

The guard at Walter's side closed his eyes and opened them, looking right at Simon, much as a cat will, in silent confidence. It was a communication of friendship, and did much to offset Walter's tone. The solidly built attendant was evidently a knight—his leather body armor was of the highest, supple quality, and the bridge of his nose was lightly scarred from some old sword cut.

The young herald had been tugging at Walter's sleeve. He tugged again, and was ignored. The herald spoke up on his own, perhaps to compensate for his master's abruptness, "Walter Tirel, by the grace of Jesus the Lord Count of Poix, extends his greetings."

Walter silenced this flowery announcement with a slap—not hard, but loud—across the boy's leather cap. "Hush, Nicolas," he said.

Trembling inwardly, but with what he trusted was an outward calm, Simon kept his place at his mother's side. Introductions were a source of conflict, and many men fell to bloodshed because no one could establish who had the right of way on the road—or which lord had the right to demand livestock from a householder.

"A horse like the one you gave Prince Henry," added Walter Tirel. "I will have one, too."

Simon had endured enough aristocratic high-handedness for one day, but he was careful to speak evenly. "The lord prince took the stallion," he said. "He confiscated the creature, claimed it, and rode it away as a present for the lord king. It was neither a gift nor a purchase. And strictly speaking, the animal was not even mine to give away." Simon let this fact become clear, before he added, "Although of course we are honored to be able to please King William."

Walter Tirel said nothing, looking from Christina to Simon, and back.

"And if, my lord Walter," added Simon, "you have caused the death of our rooster, we will be pleased to have a new breed fowl from the king's flock."

"Marshal Roland," said Walter doggedly, "reported that you were horse-rich, with a dozen stallions to spare. Bertram," he added, turning to the knight nearby, "is that not what he asserted?"

Bertram, the knight, was clean-shaven, with a head so closely cropped as to appear nearly hairless. He put a hand on the brass-and-leather pommel of his own weapon and made a show of looking etched with grim purpose. But there was a quality in the man-at-arms's eyes, a touch of smiling embarrassment, when he allowed, "My lord, that is what the lord marshal chose to make us believe."

Simon said, "The lord marshal was, if you will forgive me, badly mistaken."

Walter blinked, uncertain, and at a loss for words. He smoothed the softly woven folds of his cloak and adjusted the agate signet ring which he wore over his leather glove.

"What is he saying?" inquired Walter of his herald, although Simon's Norman accent had been the exact replica of the best speech on either side of the Channel.

"My lord," said Nicolas, looking up at his master, "he means that there are no horses here."

"What?" demanded Walter.

Nicolas repeated his words.

Walter looked around at his surroundings. He opened his mouth, then shut it again.

"This is an unpleasant surprise," said Walter.

"My lord, you will dine with us," said Simon, in haste to inject hospitality into the encounter.

"I am disappointed," said Walter.

"We will enjoy a pullet, gold from the hearth," said Simon with a forced heartiness, "and some of the cheese that is a legend throughout England."

"In food," Walter said, "I have no interest."

"My lord thanks the lord and lady of this house, however," prompted the herald in a perky singsong, "for their kindness."

Walter let his eyes take in the overhead beams, and the carved boxwood benches.

"What is this place?" he asked.

He meant, belatedly: *Explain to me who you are.*

Plainly, introductions that should have been carried out by the servants had been interrupted by the death of the breed cock.

Christina had been watching Walter with a growing look of alarmed compassion, and now she put a hand on her son's sleeve to beg his silence. "My late husband was Fulcher Foldre," she said, "who struck a mastiff across the skull with his staff, defending the life of the Conqueror."

"Indeed?" inquired Walter.

"My late husband," she continued, "was granted this land by a grateful King William. My own father," she added, with a ladylike lift of her chin, modesty no virtue where a good name was concerned, "was Usher of Aldham. He killed ten Danes with the edge of his sword, and earned the gratitude of his folk."

"And I, my lord," said Simon, "hope to serve as your hunt squire as early as tomorrow."

"On whose authority?" asked Walter.

Simon saw his opportunity to hunt with the king's party fading away. He was also aware that embarrassing a nobleman could permanently cool his friendship—and perhaps even prove dangerous.

"On your own authority, my lord," said Simon, "if you desire it."

"Ah, yes," said Walter, sounding galled and unsure where to vent his anger. "We must certainly inquire what I might choose to do, and with whom."

"You were deceived, my lord," said Simon.

"Was I?" asked Walter icily.

His question was not intended to be answered directly, and Simon did not like the quality in his voice. Walter's slow-dawning ire could result in immediate violence to passing dogs, house servants, or to anyone standing before him.

"Marshal Roland tried to shame my family in sending you here," suggested Simon. His meaning, which could not be put into words, was *Go slap the marshal's face, and leave us alone.*

"Are you saying that Roland Montfort lied to me?" Walter inquired frostily.

"I will not slander the royal marshal," said Simon. "He sent you here without telling you exactly who we are."

"Why would he choose to embarrass both of us?"

"This is a question more fit for Roland's ears," said Simon. "The royal marshal is a tireless defender of the king, but he bears me no love. And, my lord, he may intend no great respect for you."

Walter did not move.

At last he said, "I see."

Simon was in suspense, doubting that Walter would prove to be a man of peaceful humor. A man of high name would be easily forgiven if he butchered a man of somewhat lower station for insulting a royal marshal.

Simon was not surprised when Walter began beating his mantle, searching his belt, determined to locate some weapon, there could be no doubt.

"Your purse, my lord," said Nicolas, holding up a leather bag secured with many knots. Again, he had to tug hard at his master's sleeve to get his attention.

"Pay this man—" Walter began.

He paused, and corrected himself. "Recompense this noble lady and her son, lord of this place, for the breed stock we have killed. And for the horse the prince took, and for their patience. Yes, pay one of those big pieces."

"This is evidence of a giving heart, my lord," said Simon. A flat disc of precious metal extended between the herald's fingers, catching the muted light.

Outside a wealthy abbey church, gold was rarely seen, and silver was sufficient for even the deepest debt. Simon did not touch it. "And too generous. But Swein the horse breeder will enjoy your kindness—I'll be pleased to pass on your compensation. And he'll perhaps provide you with a willing mount in return."

"He will?" Walter asked. "Do you think so?"

The herald put the coin back into the purse, where it fell into place with a soft, subterranean sound. "I'll see that this breeder of horses is well paid, my lords."

Something about Walter prompted Simon to add, with a dash of impishness, "And as for poor Sangster, his death proves you'll be a lucky huntsman tomorrow, and we make the rooster's *corpus* our gift to you."

If Simon had misjudged Walter's character, this was when his mistake would be clear. The man's manner had suddenly reassured Simon—but it was not too late for the Norman lord to take fresh offense and demand blood or coin.

"You mock me," said Walter.

So there it is, thought Simon. *Here is sure proof that I have talked my way into trouble.*

And yet Simon would not allow himself to apologize at that moment, or to offer so much as a smile. If there was going to be violence here in his own home, surrounded by the walls of his ancestors, he would not take a single step back.

Although, in his heart, he might wish to. Simon gave a hopeful glance at the young herald, and then met the eyes of the man-at-arms. The herald was admiring the square of tapestry on a far wall, precious needlework Christina had sewn in the early years of her marriage, a silken dove with its wings outspread. Bertram was smiling with his eyes, sending Simon a silent reassurance.

Walter smiled.

"I have been a fool," he said with a laugh. "And you have offered me your patience."

Simon smiled, too, the tension in the hall lifting, rising upward with the lingering hearth smoke.

Walter did something then that surprised Simon and melted the last of his anxiety.

The nobleman took Simon's arm, in a gesture of friendship. It was not simply a sign of warmheartedness, Simon knew, but an act for servant and companion to see.

Walter said, "Simon, I'll enjoy hunting with you."

· 8 ·

SIMON WAITED UNDER THE ENORMOUS chestnut tree.

Foldre came from an old word meaning thunderbolt. Simon had sometimes wondered what forefather on what Frankish heath or tideland had earned this forceful name. He had to imagine a rattling storm, sheep panicked, pigs all a-tumble, and brave or drunken Fore-*foldre* hurrying out in the flash and rumble to tie up the livestock gate.

Simon knew enough to be able to imagine that whatever courage his remote ancestor might have stumbled into, it was at least half accident. Just as today's changing fortunes were all the result of a horse with more spirit than sense, and a Norman visitor with more good humor than pride.

It was all because of Providence, or, perhaps, the design of Heaven—otherwise known as luck. He paced a rapid circuit around the giant chestnut tree, their usual meeting place. He paced around again, impatient, but with the sort of simmering impatience that must be mastered.

There was no sign of Gilda.

Gilda's cheerful, mild-mannered father Peter Shipman had been killed by the Norman knight Guy Turpin eight winters ago for not running the *Saint Bride* aground during a storm.

Guy Turpin had been a quarrelsome knight, difficult even for his cantankerous, castle-building fellow Normans. Some said that one reason William had invaded England from his dukedom in Normandy was because he had too many bristling, swaggering warriors on his hands and not enough for them to kill.

Guy Turpin in turn had drowned in a ferry accident far off, on the river Ept. Some said that a sword wound was found under the knight's ribs. Simon believed that a hunger for revenge remained in Oswulf's breast to this day, coiled and dangerous, and that Gilda shared some of her brother's sentiment.

What a noisy countryside it was, swine and cows, sheep and Swein's horses all bickering, agreeing, bedding down slowly in the long summer twilight. Hens, bereft of Sangster, clucked and scolded, and a woodcock in the chestnut high above broke into its far-carrying, liquid song, *You're lucky, yes you are.*

An ox was stuck, bellowing for help, one of Plegmund's brutes. The poor beast's call went out into the lingering twilight, a mindless but understandable bawl. Even this repeated bellowing made Simon realize how much he loved this place, this splendid tree, these green, muddy acres all around.

And how much he longed to see Gilda.

Simon wished that he could create a song like the one he had heard one market day, the verses of the riverbank, forgiving the doe for cutting its silt with her hoof.

Red sun, white moon,
What pain to me if the lady
Thus escapes the hound?

Simon always lingered when he heard a minstrel perform, and he had a good memory for the ballads he heard, including both the high-minded lover's tunes and the earthy drinking songs.

The trouble with waiting for someone under a well-known landmark was that people passing by could see Simon easily, guess why he was there, and offer their best wishes.

Abbot Denis of the nearby Saint Bartholomew Abbey hurried by, his four greyhounds straining at their leashes. They caught scent of Simon and each leaped or halted, like individual statues, stone-carved dogs instantly captured at a moment of attention, and then just as quickly loose and alive again.

"Give our best to Gilda," called the abbot with a smile.

Simon thanked him.

Wilfred the reeve, as farm managers were called, strode past with a wave. His family had worked for Simon's for generations. He carried a coil of new rope to help the drovers pull out the ox stuck in the local pond. Wilfred was an energetic, innovative man, down to instituting new foot markings for Aldham geese, so that wandering fowl might be returned. Wilfred even strode along like a man with substantial plans: new tools for the hemp beaters who made the rope, and—soon to come—new sacks for Plegmund's oats.

"A very good evening, my lord Simon," called Wilfred in his usual vigorous manner.

Simon wished him a good evening in return. He admired Wilfred. His plans cost silver and effort, creating a drain on the manor's resources, but they promised prosperity.

And Simon considered how contentedly the land around him thrived, and how little any of the creatures or human beings really needed Simon's oversight. If Simon's life was a poem, it had reached the verse in which the expectant hero rode toward a looming gate, knocked resoundingly, and met some adventure.

It was time for Simon to take on some grand undertaking. Perhaps—was it so unlikely?—he might find an enduring place in the royal court.

He prayed, *Let Gilda come quickly. So I can tell her that tomorrow I go hunting with the king.*

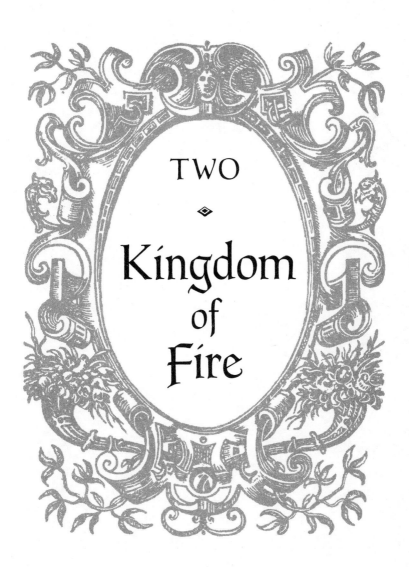

TWO

◈

Kingdom
of
Fire

· 9 ·

HE ROYAL MARSHAL ROLAND MONTFORT was happy.

He was not in this humor often, and he knew the sentiment was always fleeting. But an attractive woman sometimes made him feel this way.

"I told you I had something to show you," she said when she and Roland were safely off into the forest.

Her name was Emma, and she was a freedman's daughter—her family made charcoal for the smiths and royal chamberlains of New Forest. Her hair was tied up just so and her homespun mended and her goatskin boots newly sewn with yellow thread, all more than enough to make her look like a morsel in the eyes of the royal marshal. Her fingernails were enduringly grimed with hardwood soot, but

Roland thought her a beauty, and he had an eye for women.

She kept her hand in his, leading him onward. She had reported that she had seen something, and so she had, far out in the woods during the long summer twilight.

It was a hare caught in the nearly invisible loop of a poacher's snare. The long-eared creature struggled in the lingering light, kicking hard enough to break his neck if he kept struggling, nearly a man's height off the ground, plunging away in terror as the two human beings approached.

"You said you wanted me to watch and listen," said Emma. She spoke the Norman tongue, but her New Forest accent made the familiar words sound like a new language. "For signs of poaching," she added. "And for other things, as well."

Roland watched as a pair of wings felt the seam of air just above the greenwood, a night bird on its first hunt of the early twilight. Roland did not envy the predator, required to kill to stifle hunger. What lord prince of the forest, Roland wondered, did the white-feathered owl serve? Nagged by his conscience, Roland had been unable to shake free of the memory of the dying poacher.

It was a joyless recollection indeed. Roland believed that God allowed a lawman to kill a wide number of criminals in the pursuit of his duty, but that Heaven's Lord grew displeased if the number became too great.

The Montfort family was a long line of careful men—chandlers to lords and kings, chamberlains and advisers of judgment. Roland's background contrasted starkly with the vainglorious Tirel clan, men who would chop off a head with more facility than they could use the one God had given them. Roland would do anything to embarrass and deplete the Tirel family—and to keep their kind far from the king.

Emma kept her hand in Roland's and gave a sound like a purr, resting her head against his shoulder. The English criminal was a fearless wight, Roland would grant him that. It took nerve to set a snare so close to the king's lodge. This was an old snare, set days ago, the hare half dead from terror and starvation. The animal was bleeding between the ears where an owl had injured him moments before. How the long-eared creature had survived so long without becoming some owl's or raven's dinner was testimony to his good luck. Roland used a hunting dagger to saw at the sinew of the trap.

When the hare was released he fell to the ground. Roland had to laugh. The creature believed he was dead! The animal lay, convinced that this muted, forest dusk was the color of eternity. The marshal clapped his hands once, and the jack hare was off, bounding crazily, pausing midair, and then vanishing, only to reappear far off, frozen in flight.

"He'll tell all the other hares," said Emma with a laugh, "what an adventure he's had."

"Is that what you English believe?" asked Roland.

"Believe about what?"

"Do you think that woodland animals speak to each other?"

His question was serious—he had no idea what the English thought about anything, aside from always overestimating the power of their own flesh to withstand the ax.

"He's going to tell his hare bride how kind the royal marshal is," she said, "how handsomely he smiles, and how his eyes sparkle."

This was rank flirtation, purest flattery, but Roland did not mind.

"Why aren't the local yeomen," asked Roland, "as pleasant as their women?"

"There are women enough," said Emma, "who would lie with you just to stick a knife between your ribs."

If Roland had a characteristic that won him any affection, it was that women—smart, quick-eyed women—sometimes found him agreeable company. But the love life of the royal court was complicated, and it was difficult to woo, seduce, and take pleasure in a creature like Emma under the king's roof.

The royal court on procession from one hunting lodge to another across the woodlands of England was a festival of drunkenness and feasting. Once it arrived at a hunting lodge, it filled the location with wine-loving, dice-playing clerks and pitcher bearers, dispensers of the larder and masters of one office or another. The king's retinue included dressers to arrange the royal clothing, scribes to write up his instructions, and even a dwarf named Frocin who recited ballads and amused the king and his companions with witless hilarity.

"I heard the miller say that you ate a human heart once,"

Emma was saying, "in Ely Green. Cut the pulsing organ right out of a rebel, and ate it on the spot."

How could folk believe such a thing? Roland marveled. How would a respectable marshal even begin to go about eating such a still-trembling human heart? A large, bloody organ, as any hunter knew well, anyone who had field-dressed a stag?

That was the problem with the English—as soon as you started to like one of them, they said or did something that stopped you. "Is that what you believe, Emma?"

"You mean, it isn't true?"

She was teasing, Roland thought. "Oh, yes," he said, "and I bit the entire head off a hayward last May Day."

Emma had the most enticing laugh. She was intrigued by her own good luck at catching the eye of the marshal, and was dazzled at her own daring at coupling with him—this would have been the third time in a fortnight. Roland had first come upon her as she planed the bark off a tree in Fulford Reach—a long, half-boggy meadow—curls of wood in her hair. She'd knife him as merrily as love him, Roland knew that. It was not a contradiction—women sometimes relished a dangerous partner, and at times men felt the same way.

A sound reached them through the forest—the sharp rhythm of horses' hooves, three or four men on horses they must have picked up south of Winchester, mounts with plenty of vigor left, spurred on by their riders.

"King's men approaching, approaching king's men," was

the lodge guards' singsong reassurance, the same stalwarts who secured the castles in Winchester and London, although far less sober here.

"Undermarshal Climenze," cried a cheerful voice in the distance. "My lord, did you drink the Thames dry again?"

Dogs set up a round of barking, both the scent hounds and the running hounds giving welcoming voice to the men returning from London. A larger dog joined in barking, the fearsome Golias—Goliath—an animal whose continuing existence in the kingdom was an annoying mystery to Roland. The marshal knew that duty required him to return at once.

But he had reason to linger. The sound of distant merriment made the forest seem all the more alive with a bracing, challenging unfriendliness—leaves shifting, unseen wings hunting, and Emma's willing, teasing companionship enticing him to stay in this perilous darkness.

And he would have stayed there—if only it were possible.

"Aren't you going to give me a reward, then?" she was asking. "For showing you that New Forest poachers aren't afraid, even this close to where the king sleeps at night?"

"You'll meet me here tomorrow evening?"

She did not respond.

"Promise me," he said.

"What if it rains?"

It would be pleasant to have a pretty smile waiting for

him at night after a day in London's hectic, duty-ridden court. With a smile and a measure of wine, even a marshal might feel he was very much like a human being, if not one graced by Heaven's favor—he had killed too many men. A wife like Emma would be the surest route to a new life and certain happiness. She'd have a meager dowry, but the warmest embrace in Christendom.

But the king would not approve of such a match—he preferred his right-hand men to be undistracted by marriage. Roland owed much to King William. When Lord Marshal Bennett tumbled down the stone steps of the Thames embankment and drowned a few summers ago, Roland had worked hard at resuscitating the jolly old drunk, pummeling his master's body, trying to pound it back to life. The effort had won the king's approval, and he had awarded Roland the signet of office right there, the gold ring still warm from Bennett's finger.

"I'll send my sergeant Grestain, Emma," he said, "to see you home safely."

"My brothers would laugh me to shame," she said, "if I showed up with a royal sergeant dogging my steps." She put her arms around him.

Emma might well have a brother waiting behind this beech tree, or that towering elm, waiting to step out with a charcoal burner's ax and split the royal marshal's head.

She had three brothers, all heavily muscled and experienced at chopping and splitting. They could have the royal marshal turned to ash by morning, with no one the wiser.

"Besides," said Emma, "upon my soul, Grestain makes me uneasy."

"Follow the high road home, Emma," he said. "Be careful."

"Whatever do you care, Roland?" she asked in return. "What if Mad Jack springs out on me and cuts me to chops?"

Roland hurried alone, back toward the smoke and murmur of the lodge, feeling the possibility of English spite from behind every shadowy tree. Their women sometimes saw the lord marshal's merit, but their men were cunning and resentful. A forest where trapper-thieves worked within bow shot of the lodge was no safe place for a king to ride.

He would warn King William again: stay in the lodge and let the cup bearers comfort you with drink.

But when did the king ever listen?

· 10 ·

"UT BESPORTING YOURSELF, MY LORD marshal?" came the query from the candle-light. "Out jigging in the bracken with a lass?"

Frocin approached, dancing a flat-footed caper, trying yet again for the impossible—to draw a laugh from Marshal Roland.

Frocin was a very small man with a large grin. Roland had long ago given up even trying to pretend to smile at his efforts. He had come to feel a subdued sort of pity for the royal dwarf, one of the king's favorite companions. Perhaps, thought the marshal, someday Frocin would do the court a genuine favor and cut his own throat.

"Where is Climenze?" inquired Roland with an air of careful patience.

"At bread or at beer," said the comic.

Roland made a show of not following Frocin's meaning.

"Over there," sighed the dwarf. He added, in a murmur, "If you would but give me a smile."

Roland knew that the glance he gave the dwarf at that moment would have frightened a hangman.

"My lord marshal," said Frocin, correcting himself, "if you would but grace me with the music of your laugh." He folded his hands on his breast and bowed so low that his absurdly shapeless cap toppled onto the floor. This was a contrived mishap. Roland's fear was that someday, while chortling at some wheezy tomfoolery like this, the king would not see the approach of an assassin.

Although Roland had to admit that the stunt with the cap was almost funny.

"I ate well in London, my lord, if I may say so," said Climenze with a grin. "Old mutton and fresh loaf, as the saying is."

Roland and Climenze sat in a corner of the lodge where they could speak in confidence, the rest of the big hall screened by sheets of canvas hung by the royal tenters for what little privacy such a place could offer. A low fire of blue and golden flame simmered in an iron brazier—fine charcoal made by Emma and her brothers, and purchased by the hundredweight for the lodge.

"Your mother and father, with Heaven's mercy," asked Roland, "are well?"

"And still grateful that the king's marshal gave a lowly lad like me a chance in the royal court, my lord, and that's the truth."

"And a wise choice it's proven to be," said Roland.

Climenze waved off this compliment. He had a long, agreeable countenance, like a reliable horse. "My old father can still hoist a dray mule," said Climenze, his language a sort of Norman debased with the occasional English verb. *Hoist.* No one in Paris had ever heard of such a word.

"I am sure the skill proves useful," said Roland, recalling the skinner's yard near Cripplegate, carcasses of plow horses flayed and gutted, suspended by hooks the size of anchors. Men greasy with their work bawled out instructions in a language peculiar to their trade, and the youthful Roland had helped block-and-tackle the work-emaciated hulks of oxen up into the skinner's workplace, for fun—until his father forbade it, saying it was no sport for a gentleman.

"But even my deaf father, my lord," said Climenze, "has heard the talk of unsettling signs."

"Do we believe in omens, Climenze?" asked Roland, keeping his conversation artful, but inwardly alive with curiosity. "Or are we rational enough to trust our wits?"

"There is an unsettling occasion in London, my lord marshal," said the undermarshal, resorting to the official language of clerks to make himself clear, and to determine that his superior took his report seriously.

"There is always some brew-house riot," said Roland,

fond of the big town, and wishing he were there.

"You're right as to that," said Climenze with a knowing smile. "But this is something new in the way of troubling indications, my lord marshal, if I may put it so."

Roland liked Climenze. This was the man he sent to warn the local goatherds to pen their livestock when summer was high. An injured peasant left a gap in the harvest, a skill missing during harness mending, and a strong pair of arms when it was time to beat the fields for hares. Climenze could punish—but not too severely.

Climenze, however, had been a man of enigmatic habits recently. He had taken to vanishing for hours, and showing up for duty with the perfume of expensive wine on his breath. Something warned Roland now. *Don't trust him.*

A soft-voiced intruder, with a quiet step, startled the two of them.

"Ask him what sort of troubling indications," urged Prince Henry, entering the circle of light cast by the nearly smokeless coals. The two stood and gave a bow at the approach of the prince, and Henry gave a smile and a nod in return.

Roland was surprised. "Do you know my man Climenze?" he asked.

"Indeed," said the prince, "I know your undermarshal to be as capable with the bow as he is in the saddle."

Roland would have thought Climenze was far better with ax or pike than he was at archery, but he was flattered that the prince took notice of one of his men.

Flattered, but puzzled. In the daily life of the royal court, a prince and an undermarshal would know each other by sight, but conversation between them would be rare. Roland did not enjoy this sort of by-the-way surprise. He counted on knowing men and what they were likely to do.

At this time of night—late, with nearly all the dining tables and benches broken down and cleared off—the prince was almost always stupid with drink. This night, however, Prince Henry was apparently sober.

Climenze did not speak until Roland lifted his forefinger, granting permission.

He said, "The dogs, my lords, have vanished from the city streets."

The prince gave the short, silent exhalation that was his version of laughter.

"God's teeth, Climenze, this is a sure calamity. The dogs are gone! Let us fly to our ships!"

"The dog packs have disappeared entirely?" asked Roland.

Packs of large mongrels had plagued the streets of London in recent months. They roamed only at night, and had the effect of discouraging nightwalkers—beggars and wandering lunatics. Even so, they impeded horsemen in the early-morning hours, disturbing even the bravest steed with their barking and slavering. The king, it had been generally agreed, would have to order a slaughter of the dogs before winter.

"Every last pup, my lords," said Climenze.

"Only a fool trembles at every unsettling rumor," said the prince when he and the marshal were alone.

"This is not an omen, my lord prince," said Roland. "This is evidence."

The prince stepped over to the heavy linen cloth separating them from the main atrium of the lodge. Such cloth barriers provided but scant privacy. He peered, making sure no one was listening, and then froze.

He put a finger to his lips.

The prince whisked the cloth aside, overturning a three-legged stool with a clatter. A sleeper somewhere stirred, but no spy was disclosed by the candlelight.

"I thought I heard someone," said the prince. He shrugged and gave a little laugh, like a man relieved he did not have to use a weapon after all.

"Evidence of what?" asked the prince, encouraging Roland to continue.

"Before we left the city, I ordered two dozen new pike shafts," said Roland.

"And?" asked the prince.

"The armorer told me none could be found," said Roland, soft-stepping to the very edge of the illumination cast by the steadfast candles. "There is a shortage of ash wood and hazel in London."

The prince looked at the drinking cup in his hand. He thought for a long moment, and then swallowed his wine.

"My dear Roland, London's wives have no doubt broken their sticks beating their wayward husbands."

"By the dozen, my lord prince?"

"Do you think some conspirator," said Prince Henry, "has bought up every wooden shaft?"

"To make pikes and spears—that is exactly what I believe. And this secret enemy has killed off the dogs, my lord prince, to clear the streets for fighting."

"Who would he be, this troublemaker?"

"Not a common Englishman, I think," said Roland. "Not in London. We have them well beaten in the city, although they still test their fangs in the countryside."

"Who, then," asked the prince, "is the conspirator?"

· 11 ·

ANY NUMBER OF NOBLE SCHEMERS WERE likely suspects, thought Roland—Norman barons and newly minted English dukes. The throne of England had been a prize for the taking for a hundred years, and no doubt some grasping men felt it was ready and waiting for them now.

But Roland did not voice any of this. He kept his own counsel, believing a judicious silence was his wisest course. Somewhere off in the drowsy hunting lodge, someone was getting sick, disgorging a day's worth of wine or west-land cider. The sound ceased, and the lodge was quiet again.

The prince, Roland thought, did not much resemble his brother.

The king was red-haired and ruddy-cheeked, and expressed nearly every feeling—from glee to anger—with some variety of laughter. The prince, however, spoke in even tones, with a searching, sideways glance. He liked to make other men laugh, but he rarely smiled himself.

"Marshal Roland," said Prince Henry, "you would make a challenging enemy."

This sounded like a compliment, but Roland felt a chill.

"I am loyal to my lord the king," said the marshal. He meant: *I am no conspirator*.

"And when," said the prince, "under Heaven's mercy, my brother comes to die, you will still owe the same duty to the throne."

Roland was appalled. Such mention of a monarch's death was never so brazenly voiced, even by a brother of the king. This was a trap, Roland realized—a test to discover his possible disloyalty.

"Our king is in spitting health, my lord prince," said Roland, adding, "God be thanked."

Henry's gaze was steady. Roland felt his soul being weighed, marred specimen though it was. I should not have killed the poacher, thought the marshal. *Henry did not like it then, and he does not like it now.* The prince, thought Roland, was one of those quiet, unforgiving men.

"What if I myself," said the prince, "ordered the dogs slain and the pike shafts readied?"

"I would be required to report as much to the king."

The prince laughed quietly. "Of course, I was speaking only to test you," he said.

"You are cunning, my lord prince."

"Do you enjoy bloodshed, Roland?" asked the prince in the tone of someone considering a matter of philosophy.

"In past years I did very much, my lord, but no longer."

"Would you wish for a more peaceful season, dear Roland?"

This was true enough—Roland would be glad when his life became serene, the way his father's had been. His father had been the royal chandler, with responsibility for the king's candles, but the job had a status beyond that of simply providing illumination for the long winter nights. Chandlers were generally reliable and respected men, attended by cheerful and efficient servants.

His father had been full of praise for the ancestral home of Montfort, refuge of scholars and holy men, and how finely scented the beeswax of that place had been and how softly woven the wicks. His father could pass by the heads of a dozen men on pikes, gaping and eyeless, ignoring them because his heart was full of nostalgia for Candlemas as it had been celebrated in his boyhood.

In Roland's view, the English were lucky to learn Norman ways. Not long ago a goose girl who lived in a hole in the ground near the river, a pathetic hovel, accepted a quarter silver penny to lie with him. A quarter of a penny could buy a flock of geese, a goose girl, and a bushel basket for the eggs,

but in his tenderness he had felt a generosity, and was just settling in with the lass when young Simon Foldre had stumbled
across them.

The young woman had all but screamed *rape!* and hurried
off with his silver piece, and Roland had had to endure Simon
Foldre's challenge. Simon was not altogether a useless young
man—he was half Norman, after all. And he was tall and well
built—no easy opponent. He had a way of pronouncing the
Norman words and vowels with superlative care, as though
aware that at any moment he might be exposed as what he
really was—a hare raised by cats.

"I shall ride to London at dawn," said Henry decisively,
"stopping first in Winchester to drink new ale."

With a stab of regret, Roland realized how much he wanted
the prince where he could watch him.

Roland gave a dutiful bow. "But the king will be better
defended, my lord prince, with you by his side."

"Nonsense," said Prince Henry. He laughed. "I need to
find out how it is that the rats of the Fleet River have grown
big enough to eat dogs."

"You heard about that butchery in Boulogne, my lord,"
said Roland. "Lord Walter of Poix, our Norman friend, had
to endow a very large window of stained glass to escape the
Church's censure."

"You don't like Walter, do you?" inquired the prince.

Surely the prince had heard the minstrels sing, "The man
ahorse and the man afoot met upon a bridge." The rhyme

was most offensive to Montfort pride—the Tirel hero of the song pissed on the unhorsed Montfort. That was what passed for humor in these troubled times—no sober Christian could smile at such a lyric. Roland was not sure, but he was willing to wager that he had heard the dwarf whistling the tune just last week.

"I think we need not fear the lord of Poix," said the prince. "His grandfather had a mastiff who could eat candles."

Sometimes Roland was convinced that the king and this brothers could not be spoken to as a man would speak to another, rational soul. Their minds were a mystery—even the best of them uttered nonsense. "Candles, my lord?"

"He ate twelve church tapers at one sitting, and my own uncle lost a silver shilling wager."

"That certainly does burnish Walter's name," said Roland, with an irony lost on the prince.

Perhaps the prince had been right. Perhaps someone was listening. A footstep whispered among the rushes strewn across the floor, and a cloth nearby moved, its neatly arranged folds shifting, settling.

It was Roland's turn to seek out a spy, but the royal marshal had far better cause for his suspicions.

He whisked aside a hanging drape, took a long stride through benches arranged along the wall, and seized a slight, cringing figure by the arm.

Just as he smelled the unmistakable stink of burning rushes.

The lodge was on fire.

· 12 ·

"I PUT THE FIRE OUT MYSELF, MY LORD," said the youth as Roland dragged him, kicking aside a bench in the darkness.

The apparent spy was a boy about the size of a mouse. He wore expensive lamb's wool, his yellow tunic stitched with red silk. A candle stub thrust into his belt gave Roland insight into the source of the nascent blaze.

"What are you doing?" demanded Roland.

"My lords," began the youth, "if it please you—"

Roland shook him so hard his teeth snapped together.

"By Heaven's mercy," said the lad, "I am Nicolas Durand, herald to Walter, lord of Poix."

Roland had seen the lad earlier, but the boy had remained carefully shielded by man and horse, a subtle creature who knew how to keep out of the way of his more boisterous fellows.

"Why are you spying on us?" asked the prince on his own behalf, in a voice made all the more sinister for being soft.

"I swear, my lords—" The herald caught himself, and began again. "I swear my lord prince," he said with a bow, "and my lord marshal, that I sought the ease of a chamber pot. And I lost my way."

"Did you set the lodge on fire with that candle stub?" asked Roland. The rush-cloaked floors of hunting lodges were notoriously flammable, and smoldering wicks and spilled lamp oil combined with oily filth to burn down many a fine peaked roof.

"I came upon a smoking heap of straw, my lords," said Nicolas, "and, if you will allow me to be brief, I did drown the spark with piss, and that's an end to your trouble."

Roland marveled at the boy's self-possession. This was another point of annoyance about the old-country nobles—their servants were circumspect and efficient, while Roland was lucky if his cook back in London could pluck a hen. If Nicolas was indeed a spy, he was good at it, the very picture of abashed innocence—and he was adept at putting out fires, too.

"Did you catch the drift of our plot," said Roland, "to cut off the ears of every foreign herald?"

Nicolas had the good sense to laugh at this, recognizing a hunting-lodge jest when he heard it. "My lords, I have been too well trained to allow myself to overhear what any two English gentlemen might be saying."

"We're not English," said the prince.

"We're as Norman as you are," said Roland.

"Ah," said Nicolas, too polite to disagree with two men who were plainly mistaken.

Roland sent the herald off to his night's rest with the caution that New Forest bedbugs were the size of badgers.

"Watch that lad," said the prince when the two were alone again. "He may drown fire with his bladder, but I think he hears the wind's counsel." It was said that secrets and muttered slurs, curses, and barely breathed confessions were all carried on the night air. He added, "I don't trust him."

"His dagger handle was inset with opal stones," marveled Roland.

"Walter of Poix," said the prince, "could afford to outfit his herald with a dagger of nonpareil pearl. And Walter has a sixteen-year-old sister named Alena, who I have heard is every bit as pretty as her dowry. Walter provides her with a wardrobe of silk, they tell me, although Alena is much given to prayer and—so I hear—prefers the songs of minstrels to the bloody-handed menfolk of Normandy."

"With a brother like Walter," suggested Roland, "I might prefer music to men, as well."

Walter's parents were both dead, Roland knew, and

Walter was reputed to be protective of his sister and jealous of any man who glanced her way. Some said the young woman was destined to be the wealthy patron, and welcome member, of a religious order. In a world of quick swords and ready revenge, many men and women took refuge in God. Abbeys and convents were well populated with gentlefolk who chose an ordered, contemplative way of life.

A servant dressed in the royal livery, a blue tunic and a gold-stitched cross at the breast, appeared in the flickering candlelight. The cut of his cloth cap showed him to be one of the chamberlain's men and a keeper of the king's private quarters.

"The king says he heard anxious voices, my lords," said the attendant. "And he thought he smelled fire."

The servant spoke well enough, Roland thought, but there was polish missing from the youth. The English-born young men like this one were taller than their elders, but bigger-boned and heavier-featured. Their accents were becoming strange.

Roland approached the king's chamber feeling like a hound anticipating the lash.

But like a dog, Roland was devoted to his master, beyond all hesitation. He followed the chamber servant, off through the smoky shadows of the lodge. Troubled by nightmares, and gifted with keen hearing, the king never slept well. It was said that the king could hear ants tiptoe in the larder, and guess their number.

What will I tell the king? Roland wondered.

Sleep with Heaven's peace, my lord king, he would say. *No one means you any harm.*

But you should decide against tomorrow's hunt.

N HIS RETURN FROM HIS PARLEY WITH the king, Roland found Climenze once more, sitting on a bench in the far corner of the lodge, his elbows on a table as he cut the rind off a wedge of cheese.

The undermarshal stood, as was proper, but Roland waved him back to his seat, and joined him at the table. Roland accepted a slice of the fragrant cheese.

It was the delicious Aldham specialty, creamy and richly flavored. Eating gold-crusted cheese late at night like this, Roland could heartily believe that God loved the world.

Except that Roland knew too much about kings and their kingdoms to think much, beyond the moment, of divine grace. Roland said, "Climenze, you must stay near the prince tomorrow."

Climenze wiped his mouth on the back of his hand. "With pleasure, my lord," he said. "Do you need help opening that chest?"

Roland had gotten up and tugged the ironbound box out into the candlelight and was opening the strongly built container. The chest yielded. He sorted through chain mail gloves, dark with packing oil, and a collection of dirks and daggers, horn-handled and honed sharp, dangerous to the hasty hand in such light.

"Take a few men with an eye for peril—Aubri, with the broken nose, and Augustin," Roland continued. "I fear there will be trouble."

"From what quarter, my lord?"

I wish I could say, thought Roland.

"You will accompany the prince at dawn," continued Roland. "See that he rides unhurt to Winchester."

"As you wish, my lord," said Climenze. He added, "Prince Henry has few enemies." *Unlike the king,* his glance seemed to add.

"Watch the prince closely," said the marshal.

Because, he could not add, *the king does not trust him.* But Climenze was already too far lost in wine to be much of a companion. Or was there something else that made the undermarshal's gaze slip away from Roland's?

When Climenze left Roland's presence, his place was taken by the marshal's personal sergeant, Grestain.

No man of importance was ever left alone, solitude being

thought both cruel and impractical. A message might need to be sent, or some information confirmed, and despite the sleepy blinking of his eyes, the sergeant's bearing was that of ready service, one hand on the pommel of his sword.

The marshal's men were outfitted in livery much like the house servants, but with coarser cloth, their rough-woven blue surcoats decorated with gold crosses along the hem, fabric made to fit over chain mail and stand up to brambles and sword thrusts without shredding. Roland cast an eye over Grestain and found only his glove to be out of repair, a finger protruding from the soft-cured pigskin.

Roland indicated this flaw, wiggling a finger with a frowning playfulness.

Grestain's broad face colored, and he shifted his feet self-consciously. "I'll have it mended before the hunt tomorrow, my lord."

"What happened?"

"No need to concern yourself, my lord."

"Grestain," insisted Roland, his voice low and intense, "tell me what misfortune befell your hand."

"I had trouble with that dog again, my lord, just after we got back from the woods."

Grestain had stood watch at the edge of the forest as Roland enjoyed Emma's charms, and he had held his tongue from a distance when Simon and Roland had their brief, dramatic confrontation over the goose girl weeks before. Roland had no secrets from his sergeant.

"What sort of trouble?" asked Roland.

"The yellow *alaunt* called Golias," said Grestain, "with the spiked collar, tried to bite me as I passed into the lodge." An *alaunt* was a solidly built, large-jawed hound, prized for guard duty. The notorious Golias was a heavily built brute of more strength than good sense.

Indeed, judging by the red gouges along the exposed finger, Golias had succeeded in setting teeth into the royal sergeant. Roland was bitter, reflecting on the undeserved license this dog enjoyed. He was a favorite of the *lymerer*—the chief dog handler.

The *chiens hauts* were running dogs like the greyhound and harrier breeds, bred for lean swiftness and admired by the marshal. Everyone liked those high-spirited, friendly dogs, considered by most folk to be the finest of God's creatures. Golias was loved by no one, save the *lymerer* himself.

From his wooden chest, Roland tugged out the folded leather shape of what looked like a man's hollow torso. Stretched out on the hard-swept earthen floor of the hall, the cured skin slowly erected itself, shoulders assuming a shape, chest filling out. Years before, Roland's father had ordered this body armor crafted in Cheapside, where the best leatherworkers plied their awls. A father was proud to have a son joining the royal court for service with a sword, but privately worried, too.

There in the candlelight was the place on the breast where a spear had scored the leather during that violent winter in the north, chasing down rebel farmers near Tadcaster. The brass studs were still bright there where the long iron spearhead had gouged them.

"My lord, you will be careful," said Grestain, "during tomorrow's hunt."

It was common for Roland's rough men to share concerns for each other, despite their experience with violence—or perhaps because of it. Indeed, in most castles and great houses, to Roland's knowledge, a harsh life was softened and made endurable by the regard of man for his master and friend for friend.

"There will be no hunt," said Roland, "if the king takes my counsel."

There at the bottom of the trunk was a short-handled battle-ax—just the weapon he needed now.

· 14 ·

HE AX HAD BEEN A PRESENT FROM
Roland's London neighbors when word spread
that the young man who loved skinner's yards
and their rough songs had at last found a voca-
tion equal to his potential.

It had not been an inexpensive gift—iron was a valuable
mineral, beyond the means of many honest people. But in
Roland's years of increasing responsibility, he had rarely called
upon it before this moment.

He bid Grestain to come along—the law and common
practice preferred a witness when the king's justice was
enforced. Roland carried the ax head-down through the sleepy
lodge, past cloth partitions, snores, and the slow breathing of
slumber on all sides, Grestain following closely, as such offi-
cers were trained to do, without question.

Just outside the side entrance to the lodge was the dog-keep, where the sawdust was freshly strewn and the trough kept full of fresh water. As Roland unfastened the gate to this enclosure, a guard in the distance began a startled "Who's there?" but then settled for "Good evening to you, lord marshal."

The *lymerer* slept with his charges, on a bunk at the far end of the rows of wicker pens. The long, narrow enclosure smelled sharply of dog—dog fur, dog breath, a companion-able odor. Roland knelt and fetched a good-sized ox bone from among the selection of well-chewed hocks and ribs from the chips of wood on the ground. He carried the bone in his left hand, like a treat for a favorite pet.

A pack of hounds for fox and other running quarry con-sisted of twelve running hounds and the *lymerer* to manage them, and for a stag hunt a smaller pack of lean dogs who were trained to be carried on horseback. More than a score of eager dogs awakened as the marshal passed their sleeping pens, the just-stirring dogs putting out their snouts. The most veteran of them sniffed the air, whining as they nosed the iron weapon and anticipated blood.

There was a throaty growl from the far end of the dog-keep, Golias rousing just as the *lymerer* himself was awakening.

The man called, in English, "Who is that?"

Golias barked, and showed his teeth as Roland drew near. Roland recognized the call of duty, the dog setting his legs and barking with increasing vigor. The marshal felt a flicker of compassion for a beast that could have served a more disciplined master for many years yet.

The marshal thrust the bone at the thick-necked dog, and Golias seized it in his teeth. Roland brought the blunt side of the ax down in a single, swift blow, and the dog was flat, four legs out, his tongue caught in his jaw and bitten nearly in two.

One more blow, for mercy, and Roland was done.

The *lymerer* fell to his knees, his hands over his face as the dogs yapped and whined nervously, startled by this fatality among their brethren. Roland wished he knew the man's name—this sort of unpleasantness always went more smoothly if you knew the Christian name of the individual, and something about his father's trade, and his mother's family. This was one of those new English freemen, added to the treasury rolls in recent months to fill the needs of the rambling, rapacious court.

"If, before Heaven," said the *lymerer*, now in the courtly tongue, "you would spare my life, my lord, I would be grateful." He spoke the bastard language, Norman words with English sounds, that Roland heard everywhere.

"Why would I kill you?" asked Roland. It was appalling the way his reputation painted him as monstrous, even among the royal company. "Unless you yourself bite the hand of one of the royal guard, my man, your life is safe."

"It is cheerless, though, is it not?" Roland heard himself say as he and Grestain made their way back to the lodge.

"Cheerless, my lord?" asked the sergeant.

Roland caught himself. A marshal did not think out loud, even before his trusted sergeant. But it was cheerless, in truth—this and all the killing to come.

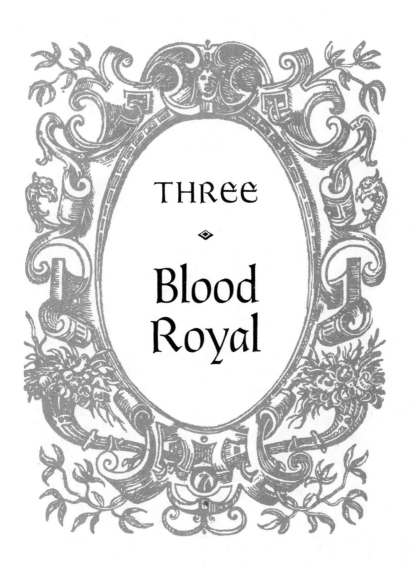

THREE

◆

Blood
Royal

· 15 ·

"I PRAY THAT TODAY'S HUNT, SIMON," SAID Christina, "will bring us long-due honor."

Simon knew that his mother had a practical view of his future. With many English folk of name beginning to rise to positions of influence under the Normans, her son was wise to curry the favor of the king.

She gave Simon a kiss, and as he climbed into the saddle, she gave him a hand up, briefly supporting his weight as capably as any man. In the predawn dark, the family home gave off an inner glow.

As eager as he was to be off on the day's adventure, he had a sudden, surprising yearning—why not stay here where he belonged? His home had never looked so safe and peaceful. Alcuin, the chief houseman, gave Simon a reassuring smile from the broad doorway. Simon thought he had never seen the worthy retainer looking so well.

"Have no fear, my lady," Certig said with a laugh. "We'll have Simon back again by nightfall, whole and hale."

"School the king in mercy, Simon," advised Christina with a quiet laugh, the way she would have said, *Teach Caesar the billy goat to speak Latin*.

Simon had slept fitfully, only to dream of hare and fawn, poachers' snares, and silently screaming yeomen. Now as he rode beside Certig, he chewed bay leaves. Such herbs were thought to sweeten the breath and disguise human scent from the quarry.

As the two passed the bend in the river, the *Saint Bride* lay careened on the green river stones. She was still above the waterline, two figures working in the early light, Gilda and her brother no doubt readying the ship for a merchant voyage.

Maybe, Simon thought, Gilda will look up from untangling the ropes and take in the sight of me in my green cloak and hood, off on a royal hunt. Her brother might not approve, but even he might say to himself, *Look at Simon, setting forth on a hunt!*

Simon had waited into darkness the night before, but Gilda had never arrived. Simon realized after a long vigil that her brother had convinced her that Simon was not a worthy companion. Simon seethed inwardly as he imagined Oswulf's counsel—that Simon had done nothing to save Edric's life, and that Simon was too much the Norman swain in any event for a river man's daughter.

"I'm happy I'm not a river dweller," said Certig, thoughtful enough to distract Simon from his disappointment—neither sister nor brother looked up from their work. "It's a life of salt blisters and storm."

"No doubt," said Simon appreciatively. "I am sure we are lucky to abide with foals and sucklings."

He had only sailed on the *Saint Bride* once, when a freight ship from Utrecht foundered off Portsmouth—disappeared with a cargo of wine. Simon had shipped with Gilda and her brother in an attempt to rescue sailors from the sea. The freighter had left not a spindle on the tossing, fuming brine. Since that brief, sad voyage Simon had thought sailing an adventuresome life, but unforgivably dangerous.

Simon and Certig rode in companionable silence until they were not far from the royal lodge. The sounds of a smith's hammer reached them through the trees, and dogs yapped excitedly.

Simon pulled the reins, halting his horse. "Hold on a moment, Certig. I see something extraordinary."

"Do you see Mad Jack?" inquired Certig with a laugh—a nervous, unhappy sound.

Simon gave a chuckle. Mad Jack had been a freeman living

upriver, the stories told, where the waters were shallow. One day a jealous spirit entered Jack, enticed by the sight of his wife gossiping by the well with a passing jongleur. Jack killed his wife, chopped her with his ax, and ran off into the greenwood. Legend held that Mad Jack ate children and had a long, moss-green beard.

Now Certig was laughing again, but with increasing anxiety. "Don't leave the road, Simon."

Simon retrieved the wonder he had spied by reaching through the leaves, closing his hand around it, and gently tugging.

He freed his discovery from the branches of the oak.

"That is a sure sign of luck," breathed Certig.

Simon handed the discovery to the servant with care—a wide-spanned antler, gracefully pointed, a trophy lost by a rutting stag. It was only one half of a buck's brace of antlers, quite possibly loosened by a mating duel and snagged on an overhanging limb.

Simon had never approached the royal lodge, and he did not particularly enjoy the sight of it now, despite his excitement at the prospect of the hunt. The Normans celebrated a style of architecture that, unlike the square, earth-and-oaken keeps of the English, could only be called arrogant.

Foreign vanity had lifted these new stone arches, and puffed-up pride had shaped these iron-spiked gates. This was a hall for eating roast venison, and for sleeping off the evening wine, and yet it was as wide and as lofty as any Jericho.

Simon had never been introduced to a king—the thought of it made him profoundly ill at ease.

"Be quick," Certig was urging. "My lord, why are you so hesitant?"

· 16 ·

SIMON FELT THAT HE HAD GOOD REASON to pause in the saddle and gather his mental powers.

A king was designated by God to be His right hand in the world. Just as a man might stretch his fingers and pick up a walnut, guess its weight and wholesomeness, so Heaven employed monarchs to sort, select, and command matters on this mortal earth. To interfere with a crowned sovereign was to stand in the way of the divine.

It was difficult to think of what to say to such a presence. Ordinary good manners could hardly suffice, and yet Simon had no range of anecdotes and funny stories with which to embellish his banter. Besides, there were tales, confirmed by honest travelers, of ears shorn from the heads of Englishmen who were slow to pay their respect in homage or silver. The monarch, Simon knew, was perilous company, and no man under Heaven quicker to take offense.

Hunts usually began very early in the day, but morning was upon them and the king did not show his presence in the outer yard. This king's absence was further evidence of the monarch's power. He could make his entire court, chandler and turnspit, horse guard and chamberlain, stand idly waiting by the hour, and not a single adviser would complain.

The anticipation had the effect of increasing Simon's apprehension all the more. Should he have stained his hunting boots with walnut oil, and was his belt too stiff? It creaked, Simon was convinced, every time he moved.

No one in the outer courtyard had more than a glance for the two new arrivals, waiting in the dawn-dappled shadows, although Simon was aware that the gate men leveled their stares, knowing who they were and not approving.

Simon sat upon a mare from his own stock, the placid Silk, named for her smooth nature, and Certig perched on ever-reliable Blackfire. There was no need for a horse of warlike spirit today. Deer hunting called for steady mounts, their placid browsing deceptive to the quarry.

"My lord," said Certig in a low voice, "I count a full score of men I have never seen before. Have you ever seen so many strangers?"

"On market day, perhaps," suggested Simon.

"Not even then," said Certig.

"You're right," agreed Simon.

Simon dismounted and made a show of nonchalance, sipping a bit of warm wine from a maple-wood cup offered by one of the servants. He made every effort to look the part of manly readiness. He had worn his forest-green hunting cloak, a gift on his last birthday from Oin. Woodland green was the preferred color for the hunt—deer were thought to possess keen eyesight, able to spy a colored sleeve or brightly decorated cap from far away.

Scent hounds panted on their leashes outside the large oak-timbered building, and foresters tugged on gloves and shared goatskins of wine, man and beast subdued but tense. The dogs sniffed and wagged and made every show of being eager.

Today's hunt was going to be a genteel but deadly game. It was not going to be a bout of field beating, like the peasant practice on common lands, laughing and thumping, driving hares out of the field to the waiting nets and clubs of boys. Nor was it going to resemble the laughing, pink-cheeked assembly gathered to ride after foxes or wolves, like the noisy company of wine-soaked royal guests Simon had watched from a distance since boyhood. Today's sport was to be more subtle.

Just then a house guard—as Simon took him to be, caped and hooded—made his way toward the two visitors.

The guard looked over Simon's cloak and boots, expressionless but quietly critical, Simon thought. But this impression of measured hostility was dispelled by the confiding whisper. "The king is still asleep, Lord Simon, and Prince Henry has ridden north on urgent royal business. My master begs your patience—he spilled wine on his hunting cloak."

With an embarrassed laugh, Simon recognized Walter's man-at-arms from the day before.

"Yes, it's Bertram de Lis, my lord," said the knight. "We hardly spoke or were even introduced yesterday, what with the misunderstandings." He lowered his voice. "I fear for marshal Roland, and that's the truth."

This news gave Simon no grief.

"Did Walter and the marshal," Simon wondered aloud, unable to hide his hope, "exchange hot words?"

"No, my lord Simon," said the knight, "but my lord Walter has a certain angry smile that I recognize."

"Oh, the two noble fellows will sit down and share their counsel," said Certig consolingly, "and your master Walter will see to it that Roland grants an apology to all concerned."

"No," said Bertram with an air of thoughtful regret, "I think that my lord means harm."

"Over yesterday's embarrassment?" asked Simon. He had to laugh. Every knight and milkmaid in England endured worse indignity, simply hearing Norman conversation in the street.

Bertram gave Simon a measuring look. "My lord, have you heard what happened to the Count of Boulogne?" he asked like a man sharing a grisly confidence.

Simon admitted that the Count of Boulogne's fate was entirely unknown to him.

Bertram did not seem unhappy to share his tale. "My lord

Walter's late brother, as Heaven willed it," he began, "was born with a crippled back. The family loved hardy little Nivard—that was his Christened name—as did all the retainers."

Simon gave a nod: *Go on.*

"Word reached us," continued the knight, "that the Count of Boulogne, a brazen drunkard, remarked that the goose he was feasting on was as wizened as Nivard de Poix."

Simon already knew enough. "I can easily imagine," he said, "what happened next."

"My lord Walter rode through the dark," the knight continued, "and I went with him. It was bloodier, my lord Simon, than you can imagine. He stalked into the lord of Boulogne's chamber, and my lord plunged his sword through the poor sot's breast, all the way to the wall."

Before Simon could make any remark, they were interrupted by an approaching voice, cheerful but insistent. "You men, if you please, will move aside."

Perhaps the brief story of the death of the Count of Boulogne inspired Simon to a certain spirit. Whatever the cause, he was in a suddenly willful mood. Perhaps it was time that a man born in England showed some aristocratic fortitude.

"We shall stand where we are," said Simon.

Certig tapped Simon's arm, an unspoken *Let's do as he says.*

· 17 ·

"I DESIRE TO STAND EXACTLY THERE," insisted the tall man in a pointed cap, "if you would be so kind as to go somewhere else."

Simon had never spoken to Vexin of Tours before this hour. He was widely known as the lover of noble ladies, and he wore his hair long and flowing, in the current fashion among men of style. He sported a pair of hunting boots with long, tapered points.

"We are sharing the morning sunlight, my lord Vexin," said Bertram, remaining where he was. "We like this spot."

"Everywhere else," said Vexin, as though instructing a man of incorrigible stupidity, "is but puddle." This was not entirely true—the dogs inhabited a dry space, and so did many of the footmen.

"Lord Simon," said Bertram, "has no more desire to plant his boots in muddy water, my lord, than you do."

Vexin lifted an artfully tinted eyebrow and tugged a long, soft leather glove from his hand. Such a gesture could be the preliminary to a challenge, and Simon's heart sank at the prospect of the day's hunt ruined by a sword fight.

"Hold, Vexin, what are you thinking?" cried a familiar voice.

Simon was delighted and relieved as Walter Tirel strode into the courtyard. He arrived with a swirl of mantle and the *click-click-click* of his agate ring against the sword hilt, keeping time as he walked.

"This," said Walter heartily as he arrived, "is my good friend Simon Foldre, who will be my right hand this day."

Vexin stood tall, and looked every inch the man who usually stood wherever he wanted. "This young Englishman is your friend, Lord Walter?"

"My very good friend," said Walter.

Vexin absorbed this. Then he gave a courteous bow and said, "I shall be honored, Simon, if you will take pleasure in that little portion of dry earth."

Vexin departed with a sweep of cape and the lingering scent of lavender perfume. Simon was grateful for Walter's intervention. He was glad to see Walter, too, not only because his arrival had interrupted a crisis. Walter's brisk humor made Simon happy. But something about Simon's new friend was melancholy now, and his smile was apologetic.

The Norman ran his eyes over Simon's attire and said, "You appear to be the ready hunter, Simon. My sister Alena asked if I might find an English lord for her companionship back in Normandy, and I thought the effort not worth making. Now I am forced to reconsider."

Simon suspected that Walter was using flattery out of mere friendliness, but the sound of Alena's name did pierce Simon with a strange pleasure.

"I would be honored," Simon said, "to meet the lady Alena."

Few Norman women, it was said, would look twice at an Englishman. But the opposite was also asserted, sometimes in the same breath: any man with a feather in his cap and a store of lovers' ballads would find Norman women warm companions.

Walter gave a smile. "Some pleasant day, perhaps." Then he leaned into Simon and added, confidingly, "The king says he will not hunt this morning."

This was disappointing news indeed.

"Why not?" Simon managed to ask.

Of course, a delayed hunt would mean that Simon could get all the more ready for the morrow. He could ride back home and stain his boots a duskier brown, and knead oil into his belt.

"He says he may forgo New Forest hunting altogether this

season," answered Walter with an air of exasperation.

"Altogether?" Simon echoed, feeling his hopes entirely dissolve.

"Marshal Roland," said Walter, "advises the king not to go forth."

"Why?"

"There are reports: violence in London, strange omens and disquiet," said Walter. "Prince Henry has been sent back to the city to resolve the trouble. At the best of times, the forest is dangerous, is it not?" But Walter was no longer paying full attention to his own words. "You found this in the woods?" he asked, reaching out to stroke the ivory points in Certig's grasp.

"Dangling from a tree," said Simon.

Walter put a finger to his lips, captured by a thought. He took the span of antler into his gloved hands.

"Come with me, Simon," said Walter.

Simon did not hesitate, leaving Certig behind with the horses.

But his heart hesitated, aware that he was leaving behind an era of innocence regarding royal matters and stepping into a richly scented, complicated future.

The interior of the lodge was strewn with fresh rushes, a pleasant sound as the dried vegetation crackled underfoot. They smelled of fresh harvest, Simon thought, just as the entire lodge was awash with the smell of new timbers and recently planed bench wood. Servants stacked disassembled furniture against a far wall, where it would be ready for the next meal, and house dogs mock-growled and sported, disputing possession of a well-chewed bone of beef.

There was an air of homelike refuge to the place that surprised Simon, despite the guards with their chiming chain mail and the richly robed chamberlain unscrolling an account on a candlelit table.

"Where are we going?" Simon inquired with a whisper.

Walter did not answer.

"Who are you taking to meet our lord king?" inquired a reedy voice.

A very small man cavorted from the shadows, and Simon knew that this could only be the famous dwarf the king kept so richly rewarded. Simon readied a laugh—the man was supposed to be the cleverest wit in England.

"Never you mind, Frocin," said Walter cheerfully.

"Kick me out of the way, then," said the small man, crouching before them, presenting his backside as a target. "Because I insist that you tell me who this is."

Walter gave a preoccupied laugh, not like a man who was actually amused, but as though laughter were requested and he did not have the heart to deny it. But he did not bother to introduce someone of Simon's good family to a creature who was little more than a servant.

Simon spoke on his own behalf. "I am called Simon Foldre, and I am honored to meet you."

He received a bow in return, with the hat doffed and waved in pretty circles through the air. Frocin was older than Simon had expected, with a white fringe around a bald pate—the deep show of courtesy cost him some physical effort.

"Ah, you have a trophy," said Frocin, upright once more. He eyed the polished splendor of the antler. "Go on in to the king—he'll be glad to see you, my lords. He is in council with Lord Iron-beak, and needs something to quicken his pulse."

Walter flung a hanging wool-and-silk barrier to one side—it caught briefly on something—and beckoned Simon with a toss of his head.

As the folds of drapery swung wide, closed, and opened again, Simon caught a glimpse of a red-haired man perched on a chair in the chamber beyond, washing his hands and nodding to whatever he was being told.

The man now drying his hands on a white linen cloth was red-haired and ruddy-featured. Simon had seen him at a distance, and recognized him. The linen retained the squares imprinted on it by the royal launderer, and the man obliterated these folds as they absorbed water from his hands.

King William looked at Simon, and looked again, observing Simon with knife-blue eyes.

Not yet, Simon wanted to protest.

I haven't readied any remark fit for the royal presence—I haven't arranged my thoughts.

"My lord king," said Walter, "look what we have found in the forest."

Simon didn't quite like that *we*.

Simon knelt, rushes crackling at his knee but his belt remaining cooperatively silent.

Roland looked on from a corner of the chamber. *Lord Iron-beak,* thought Simon with a belated inner warmth. The name was all too apt.

· 18 ·

"N O DOUBT, MY LORD KING," SAID MARSHAL Roland from his station in the corner before anyone else could speak, "the antler fell off Walter Tirel's head."

The king gave a quiet laugh. "Are you saying that our old friend Walter is half beast?"

"It's well known," added Roland, with a thin smile, "that a Tirel would rut with doe and duck alike."

Walter stood straight and stiff, and Simon did not like his icy silence. Instead of replying with a riposte of his own, or waving off the offense with a bored remark, Walter absorbed the insult with a bare shiver.

"Why did I believe you, Roland Montfort," said Walter at last, "when you said you knew a place where a warhorse could be purchased for a farthing?"

"Because you are foolish, and I say it to your face," replied Roland, "and bad company for our king."

"Easy now, Roland," said King William. "Dear Walter is our friend of many years. And as for you, Walter—you must realize that Marshal Roland finds your presence at court a corrupting influence, an encouragement for me to ride through the woods half drunk."

Walter grew tall with unspoken resentment, not at the king, but at the monarch's guardian.

"The Tirel seed produces but braggarts and crookbacks," said Roland, "while I, my lord king, rise each day simply to preserve your life."

Walter took a shocked step back at this last lash of insults, turning to one side, and Simon could sense the great effort it took the nobleman to keep from dashing across the chamber and seizing Roland in his fists.

"You are too earnest a servant, Roland," said the king, fire in his voice. "And too blunt. Apologize to my dear companion this instant."

Roland offered a handsome bow, and prayed for forgiveness from Walter before his king and before Heaven. Walter, however, glanced away, with an air of bitter reserve. Simon was sickened and troubled by the hurt he saw in Walter's eyes.

And the anger. Simon felt that it was only right to interrupt what could only become an increasingly ill-humored exchange. "My lord king," said Simon, "I myself found the stag's stately crown, and brought it to you."

"Even as Simon Foldre here made a gift to you," asserted Walter, giving Roland a further challenging glance, "of that high-kicking stallion."

Roland licked his lips, preparatory to speaking further.

"The roan," inquired King William, "that last night nearly killed my chief groom?"

"The same horse, my lord king," said the marshal.

Simon felt his plans, composed of hope and little else, falter.

"I ordered a breeder's nose cut off last month, did I not?" queried the king. "For selling me a racing mare of poor disposition."

"My lord king," said Roland, "Grestain used a paring knife to separate the breeder's visage from its prow."

Simon had heard of the badly maimed Alnoth of Bodeton. His face had swollen, and a fever kept him to his bed. Word traveled that the man's life was in doubt. For the moment, Simon wished he was far from the king and his marshal.

"A horse, like a kingdom, lord king," Walter interjected, "needs time in the bridle."

Simon appreciated Walter's remark—exactly the sort of statement Simon should have practiced and had not.

The king gave a quiet, appreciative laugh. He took the antler into his hands and examined the points of the ivory rack, pursing his lips appreciatively. "By the Holy Face, this stag must be a beauty."

"With many cousins," said Walter smoothly, "bugling and sporting, fat with summer."

"You see," said the king, turning to his marshal, "how I am tempted?"

The marshal said nothing, his gaze clouded with concern.

"How can I sit here, dear Roland," said the king, "with the eager faces of my friend Walter and this young man praying me to hunt today?"

"My lord king," said the marshal, like a man giving up a long-running argument, "I cannot promise that New Forest is in safe hands."

"No, and you cannot assert that a wen will not smite the maiden's chin," said the king, a remark which he evidently found clever, and which Walter laughed at mightily.

Roland, too, had to laugh. But then the marshal added, solemnly, "My lord king, I can only kill so many of your enemies."

"No, I don't believe that," said the king, a twinkle in his eyes. "I think you are too modest, Roland, by my faith. I think you have as many deaths in your sword as the sea has waves."

The marshal offered a dutiful but weary smile. Simon had a moment's compassion for the man of law, bound to defend the life of a monarch. Roland resembled his ruler more closely than the king's own brother did, with similar red hair.

Walter lifted a gloved finger, a man struck by a brilliant whim.

"My lord, the marshal can join us on our hunt," he suggested. "What woodland criminal would so much as nip your shin with Roland Montfort on guard as your personal varlet?"

"An excellent plan," said the king.

King William had a warm smile, and Simon wondered that, with all his power to promote cruelty and with such bitter enemies, he could be so soft-spoken. But then Simon remembered asking his father if the Conqueror had been a fierce man, with a harsh voice. His father had given a chuckle and said King William could command instant slaughter—there was no need to shout.

"You will join us, Roland," the king was saying. "I have that sweet wine from your uncle's vineyard." Every Norman was either a nephew to the others, or an equivalent crony, going back to Adam and Eve. It did not necessarily make them loving.

"Do you remember, William," said Walter, speaking to the king as a man spoke to an equal, "that time you challenged me to kill swans with my bow? They flew overhead, nine of them, between us and the sun."

The king laughed. "Yes, Walter, and you couldn't hit one of them—not with a quiver full of arrows."

"We were but boys," said Walter.

"Long-legged, and coltish," said the king, aglow with nostalgia. "And you with a squeaking new bow."

❖ ❖ ❖

Simon followed Walter across the rush-strewn hall, and into the sunny fresh air of the courtyard.

Everything had changed.

The formerly desultory, nervous, halting day was gone. It was replaced by another, brighter, crisper morning, with louder hoof clops and more eager whispers as the servants hurried. The horn blower tried an experimental *menee*—a blast of his brass instrument. It sounded sour and thin, but instantly—on a new attempt—was whole and bright, a note that captured Simon's heart.

Nicolas, the youthful herald, joined Bertram, the boy's cheeks flushed and his eyes bright. Simon was glad to see Nicolas, and greeted him.

"It is a very fine morning for a hunt, Lord Simon," agreed the herald in return. "A splendid day for a kill," he corrected himself. "If Heaven wills it."

Hounds were led off, frantic with zeal for what they knew was coming, horses mounted, final cups of wine quaffed. Roland was assisted onto a horse by one of his sergeants, as Oin the chief huntsman barked out commands. Bows were gathered, clattering armloads; quivers of goose-feathered arrows were brought forth. As slow as life had seemed in the early hours, now it was all organized haste.

Simon felt a hand on his sleeve, and he turned to meet the continuing gaze of Nicolas. "Stay close to my master," said the herald.

"Of course I shall," said Simon, puzzled by the boy's worried air. "Is there any particular threat?"

Nicolas pursed his lips. "I thought I heard plots of mayhem, but this royal court mutters when it speaks. And with such accents—forgive me, Lord Simon—I'd have better luck eavesdropping on a flock of ganders."

"But if you have cause to worry, Nicolas," said Simon, "shouldn't you tell your master?"

"My lord does not always listen to me, Lord Simon. And besides, when has danger discouraged a man like my worthy lord?"

Nicolas might have said more, but at that moment the king hurried from the lodge and sprang onto a great bay horse. Frocin cavorted in the gate yard. "Joyous hunting, my lord king," he cried. Simon was sorry to see that the comic would apparently not be joining the hunting party, but in the daylight the jester's advanced years were all the more apparent, and so was the athletic effort it took for Frocin to prance nimbly among the clattering hooves of animated horses.

Dogs trembled and danced with anticipation. They knew what the presence of the king meant, and so did every man. Oin called to the *lymerer*, a lash was cracked harmlessly but meaningfully over the heads of the pack, and within minutes they were all in the field, grouse breaking into the sky as the horses breasted the golden grass.

❖ ❖ ❖

Far off, a peasant turned and shooed his children into the family cottage. Safely on the verge of the hunting preserve, but close enough to attract royal attention, no farmer wanted to risk losing a limb or a child to the king's whim.

The feeling of prideful power was pleasing, Simon felt to his own dismay. He was one with a company that any commoner would dread, a rambling group that goose girls and millers alike would flee. The fact gave Simon a certain undeniable thrill.

But soon his attention was drawn to his personal safety. An assistant huntsman turned in his saddle and fell back to Simon's side.

"The lord king, Lord Simon," came the word, "desires a moment of your company."

Simon's horse was all too eager to catch up with the king's spirited mount.

Soon Simon rode beside the king, biting his lip lest he blurt out some artless, fatal remark.

· 19 ·

"OUR FATHER WAS A SLAYER OF VICIOUS dogs," said the king, giving Simon a long, appraising glance, "and a defender of my own father, from what Oin tells me."

"My lord king," Simon heard his own voice say, "the story can be told very tall or quite short, as the occasion warrants."

The king had a warm laugh and sounded every bit the happy monarch. His eyes were impatient, however, taking in the sight of horse and man with the keen restlessness that Simon had often observed in hunters.

"As for my father," said Simon, "I do believe that there was a wandering dog, perhaps growling, perhaps mad. My father smote it with a stick, and drove it away from the camp of the lord king your father."

Simon allowed the flourishing *smote*, his only embellishment to a legend that he wanted to share with the king in a straightforward manner. At the same time, he wished Gilda could see him just then, riding easily along as though he were accustomed to conversing with sovereigns.

"Does your father prosper?" inquired King William.

"My father was thrown by a horse," said Simon, "and died, ten years ago on the feast of Saint Anne."

The day had been hot and sweaty, dust and the fragrance of wheat heavy in the air. Certig had come running, through gleaming mirage and the ever-scribbling flies, calling *my lady, my lady* in a tone that could not be mistaken. "My father was a good-hearted man," added Simon, unsure why he felt the need to talk about his late father with the king.

"My own father was gentle-spirited, too," said the monarch, an assertion that came as novel tidings to Simon. Then the king added, pensively, "He suffered greatly from every festering humor before he died. Perhaps an instant death is a gift."

Then King William switched his horse playfully with the loose end of the reins, dismissing all sad discourse as he called for a skin of wine. He drank deeply from a goatskin handed up by a footman, and Simon drank, too, in turn.

Simon did not mention one important chapter in the life of his father. In reward for chasing off the dog, William had giver Fulcher Foldre the manor of Aldham and all its lands, making yet another loyal follower a landed duke or count—

the Normans were careless when it came to titles. It was the Conqueror's way of extending his dominion over his new kingdom.

Simon did not mention, either, that the news had killed Simon's maternal grandfather—dropped him with a stroke before he had been forced to abandon his home to a usurper. It was a tribute to Fulcher Foldre's gentle nature, and his loving persistence, that he was able, over time, to win the trust and devotion of Christina.

Simon doubted the wisdom of what he was about to say. Nonetheless—perhaps emboldened by the unusually delicious wine—he said it anyway. "Prince Henry took the horse from me, my lord king. Bel, the young fighting horse. It was no gift."

The king laughed, but this was not a friendly sound. He said, "Think of the horse as a tax."

Simon smiled grimly. Life was a hazard course of fees, taxes, duties, to be paid by service, silver, or livestock.

The king added, "You know, of course, that the steed is all but useless. I've had him stabled near the woods. Other horses make him angry, and he attacks the ostler, although he lets the hounds lick his muzzle."

There was anger behind the king's smile. But having begun this considered frankness with the king, Simon saw no reason to hesitate now. It was not the brief taste of wine rushing to his head, Simon believed. Plain speaking was a virtue—although

Simon wondered for a moment how ill any mortal would look, shorn of a nose.

Simon had not expected to mention the slain poacher, but a sudden surge of duty caused him to speak. No one else would ever have such an opportunity to honor Edric's memory.

"A man was killed yesterday, my lord," said Simon.

"Who?" the king asked, with some interest. In every report of violence, men liked to hear where the wound fell, what body part was pierced, and what weapon was involved.

Simon kept to the bare, unsatisfactory truth. "Edric, a freedman, a father and husband. And a friend to many."

"I have heard nothing of it."

Simon described the flight, the javelin, the unshriven death.

The king gave his horse a soothing pat, ruffling the bay's mane. "How far was marshal Roland from the outlaw?"

Simon did not like the course of the king's inquiry. Simon said, "Perhaps one hundred paces."

King William closed his eyes, as though picturing the javelin's flight in his mind. He glanced back, observing the marshal riding well behind, Roland watching the tree line, alert to possible harm to the royal party.

King William smiled and said, "I wish I had seen that." But then he shifted his weight, the saddle creaking beneath him. "Did this poacher owe you a debt, dear Simon?"

"My lord king," said Simon, "he did not."

"Then his death cost you nothing."

Simon could not keep the feeling from his voice. "We all thought of Edric as a neighbor. I liked him well."

The king looked away, over the windswept field they were riding across, a former pasture. Walter rode a short distance away, talking with Bertram, and Vexin of Tours was holding the reins with one hand while a servant rode beside him, brushing the sleeve of his master's cloak. The ruin of a farmer's cottage hulked among the bracken, and the road was faintly scored by old plow lines.

"Perhaps, Simon," said the king, his tone one of gentle menace, "you should teach your friends to honor their king."

· 20 ·

HE GREENWOOD WAS LOFTY, ITS FOLIAGE so thick that the blue sky was covered over. Ivy cloaked many of the trees and mantled the fallen patriarchs. Holly bushes, as large as trees, flourished in the sun breaks between the oaks.

Wild apples blushed among briars in the open spaces, and a dragonfly teased the shade, seeking, hiding, and seeking as the woodland closed in around the hunting party once more. Human voices were muted by the verdure, and amplified by it, whispers echoing, careful footsteps crashing unexpectedly among the leaf meal underfoot.

Walter and Simon were directed to a place by Oin the chief huntsman, and now that they were in the woods, Simon was aware of a further change in the temper of the day.

Walter was quiet now, his lips pressed together, his eyes downcast with some private resolve. For his part, Simon, who had always loved hearing Oin tell the legends of the hart—an animal who could grow younger with the passing years—now felt how life-giving farmland was, by contrast, with its tranquil cows and friendly herders.

The scant shafts of sunlight illuminated tangles of tiny flies. Fairy flocks, folk sometimes called these knots of insects; they believed that gnats foretold bad weather. Simon wondered whether a rain would wash out their hopes for a successful hunt. And he wondered, too, if that would be such a bad thing.

The *boisineor*—the horn blower—waited ahead of them, a silver-chased ox horn gleaming at his side. His duty would be to alert man and beast to the chase, when it was under way at last.

Oin fitzBigot handed Simon a quiver of arrows. The shafts rattled, the feathers gently brushing together. Simon withdrew an arrow and gazed upon it as though he had never looked at such a potentially deadly shaft before now.

"Your obligation," said the huntsman, "is to be as quiet as the horses yonder. When Lord Walter puts out his glove, hand him an arrow, feathered end foremost." The arrows had iron points, the metal smelling slightly of sulfur from the smith's coals. Some of the arrows were barbed; most were not.

"Simon will have no trouble," said Walter, giving his varlet a quick smile.

But the royal huntsman was nervous, many months of culling sick deer, clearing away fallen branches, and chasing off poachers culminating in this day. "I've seen barons cut by their own arrowheads, my lord," Oin replied, "and deer spooked by a footman's snicker."

"I shall not laugh," agreed Walter with mock solemnity. "And Simon will be as quiet as a wooden angel."

Walter held a bow, strung and waxed, the tall weapon graceful in his grasp. In warfare, the crossbow was the preferred weapon, but the yew bow was in fashion among aristocratic hunters.

The mounts were tethered and followed the example of the royal horse, the big bay evidently well trained at meditative grazing. Wreathes and screens of woven elm leaves encircled the horses' necks and half shielded their flanks. Bertram and Nicolas were obscure figures, and Certig, too, all in earthen brown and forest green.

To a deer, the horses would appear to be a welcoming herd. To reach the decoy horses, the approaching quarry would pass the ambush—Walter flanked by Simon on one side of the deer path, and far opposite, perhaps ninety paces away, the king and Roland. The king swept his hood back as Simon looked on, the shadow-splashed sunlight brilliant in his hair.

Simon likewise tugged off his hood, and heard a hiss from

behind a nearby tree. Oin gestured, and Simon pulled the hood back over his head. It was hard to hear very well, and the hood also constricted his view.

Simon was sweaty, and too excited to make a further sound as he peered at his surroundings. Vexin of Tours and his own varlet had found a position between the king and the decoy horses. The handsome lover of many women fussed with his bow, a silver-tipped *arcus* of such splendor that Oin must have positioned him last so that the approaching stag would not be startled.

Oin now made his way north, taking quiet steps through the leaf mold, until the huntsman could be seen no more. Simon tugged the hood away from his head, just enough so that he could hear something more than his own excited breath.

Walter lifted an exultant fist. The sound of a hunting pack could not be mistaken. Far off, their barking distorted by the undulations of the forest floor, the dogs had found their quarry.

· 21 ·

HE KING PULLED THE HOOD BACK OVER his head and conferred with the marshal, the two men side by side as the king pointed out places on the holly bush where the ground was bare.

Too often a crackling twig or leaf gave away a hunter's hiding place, as Simon had been told by regretful bowmen over cups of wine. Now as Roland and the king took their new positions on either side of the holly, Walter quietly cleared the ground where he and Simon were waiting across from them.

Simon could not tell which square-built, hooded figure was the king and which the marshal, although surely it was the king enjoying another long taste of wine from the goatskin.

Judging by the excited baying of the hounds, a promising deer was surely in flight in the woodland to the north. The dogs were not heading toward the ambush, however. Walter sighed impatiently at the sound of the muffled clamoring of the hounds, now lost, now clearly audible, but not driving any closer.

Simon knew from fireside stories that the game was never easy. The deer often sensed trouble and veered off the intended path, and sometimes took flight so successfully that the hounds could never pick up the scent again.

Even if the ambush worked, and the king and his companions loosed their arrows, and even if an iron-headed arrow or two found their target, the one or two shafts were rarely fatal. The most exciting stage of the sport would begin as the hunters followed the blood, sometimes not finding the wounded deer for many hours, through bogs and brambles, with a chance that the deer was neither fatally wounded nor even seriously hurt.

In any event, the point of the day's venture was venison. Fresh meat was often scarce, even on a king's table, and no man enjoyed the prospect of the approaching autumn, and the ensuing winter, without dreaming of a roast haunch.

Simon felt a daydream of successful feasting slip over him, the king calling for more wine and asking Simon to sing the song of the unicorn and the lion, or the one about the fox and Saint Michael, Simon elated and secure in the king's command.

And then the stag appeared.

When the deer arrived at last, he was more beautiful than Simon would have thought possible.

He was not running at top speed. In fact, the animal seemed to hesitate at the peak of every leap, as though considering whether to continue his existence as a four-legged creature or to slip into the fabric of the air and vanish.

Walter took a step forward and held back his gloved hand toward Simon. The stag stopped completely, and looked ahead at the horses, browsing among the ostler's grass, scattered beyond the leafy screens. Walter wiggled his gloved fingers, a gesture of nearly comic impatience. *Quickly.*

The arrows whispered together, a hollow clatter in the tightly woven quiver. Simon fumbled, found an arrow, lost it, and seized another, gritting his teeth with the effort to be quiet. He selected an arrow with a long, slender head and no barbs, fletched with gray-and-brown goose feathers.

The deer lifted its head and froze at this dry-bone, willow-stick noise.

They'll be singing about this for generations, thought Simon—how a novice varlet frightened off the paramount stag in England.

· 22 ·

THE ARROW WAS IN WALTER'S YELLOW glove at last, his fingers closing around the shaft. The buck had a spread of darkly gleaming antlers, and as the animal shook his head to clear his eyes of the tiny flies, Simon was certain he could hear the sound of the antlers, the points cutting through the air.

The stag took a step and then breathed in and out, a lung-expanding inhalation and a windy exhalation, much like a horse. It was hard to guess what emotions flickered in the great buck's heart, but the animal was less and less apprehensive as he stepped forward, his legs elongating and contracting, the creature stopping and starting, continuing and halting, hesitant and sure.

Walter made a small sound, nocking his arrow so that the bowstring softy twanged, like a musical string just touched by a fingertip. The deer aimed the interior of his dusky ears at the noise. The stag's forelegs locked straight, his black eyes peering directly at Walter's thickly mantled form.

The following horses then did their part, the mild-mannered steeds mounted by Oin and his men, placid pacers who approached from the rear, appearing unhurried and more interested in nuzzling the passing shrubbery than making any swift progress. But on they came, and this inverted wedge of slow horsemen emboldened the stag to reach a black hoof forward, dip his head, raise it again, and once again make his stately progress.

Walter drew his bow—not all the way, but testing it, the spruce-wood arrow squeaking faintly against the yew. The stag drew up, ears cupped again in Walter's direction, black eyes seeing where Walter and Simon stood still.

Not yet, thought Simon.

The deer isn't close enough.

He thought this even as he wanted to clap his hands together, or take a step to one side to crunch a weathered and leafless fallen branch with his foot, a wordless *fly, fly*. For some unfathomable reason, Simon wanted to warn the deer.

As though sensing Simon's desire, Walter let the air out of his lungs slowly, and then looked back at his varlet.

The character of Walter's glance surprised Simon. Walter was cool and focused, intent on this long instant of impending violence. But it was not the deer that Simon suddenly feared for most.

Walter turned to his quarry and bent the bow, the yew span trembling and then growing still with the effort. At that instant Simon sensed, in some wordless corner of his soul, that a crime was about to follow. The exact subject of the offense he could not guess, any more than he could foresee that the arrow that whipped the air as the bowstring gave out a low, sweet note would strike any living flesh.

But Simon knew that something was wrong.

Too soon, too soon, Simon would have whispered if he had made a sound.

The flight of the splinter of light made the stag shrink back, alarmed at the snapping, discordant hiss across the shadows. The arrow did not fly straight, but arced, clearly visible and then vanishing.

As so often happened in song and story, the arrow disappeared. It would be Simon's task as varlet to find it, searching among the drifts of old leaves. He followed its flight mentally right after it vanished, tracing it with his eyes.

He estimated its course all the way to the green-shrouded figure groping toward the holly bush, the sharp-edged, glossy leaves offering little support.

The hooded man faltered, one of his gloved hands finding a clasp undone on his hunting cloak, and working at it. But the stubborn attachment was not a clasp, Simon could see now. A feathered stub protruded from the heavy green cloth, and the man stumbled, falling to his knees.

HE STAG WHEELED AND DODGED THE sunlight, moving in such crisply separate, well-defined movements that he did not seem to make haste. Four hooves lofted over a heap of leaf meal, and the animal was gone.

Simon ran to give assistance to the figure he believed was the stricken Marshal Roland.

The wounded hunter fell forward, onto the feathered shaft. Simon approached swiftly, but quietly. Some part of Simon believed that if he did not startle the injured individual, then surely events could recover their balance and the arrow prove to have been tangled harmlessly in the thick woolen hunting cloak.

Simon was aware of a certain rank justice. The killer of

poachers and terrorizer of goose girls now felt the arrow's tooth.

He reached the injured man's side, Walter right behind him. Even though his instinct shrilled, *don't move him*, Simon knew that the only hope was to take the weight off the projectile at once. Simon pushed the injured man over as the hood fell away.

Simon closed his eyes and opened them again. His mind tried to make sense out of what lay before him. But thoughts would not come. All that Simon knew for certain was that this was not the marshal.

The king lay sprawled on the forest floor, his eyes half open, like a man trying to recall a dream. Blood was soaking darkly into the fine weave of the hunting cloak, and a small, dainty jewel of scarlet appeared at the king's lips. The arrow had snapped off, the feathered end dangling, red now with blood.

The king's quiver had spilled, arrows scattered across the forest floor. The stocky bow with its resin-dark string lay nearby, like instruments briefly set aside. Surely the king would wake up, call for his bow, and command that someone pick up his fallen arrows.

But after watching the death of Edric the day before, Simon had become more proficient than he had ever wanted to be in recognizing mortality. He put his hand on the king, but the absence of breath and pulse was not necessary to tell Simon what he already knew.

He also knew that Walter was in very great danger.

Simon was in peril, too.

With the death of the king, Simon thought, the king's men could not be blamed for cutting down Walter, Simon, the servants, and the horses they had ridden that morning. As a half-English interloper, furthermore, Simon would be especially suspect. What Englishman, after all, could be trusted?

Simon felt a recognition beyond fear, a giddy, clear-sighted understanding.

"Ah," said Walter, the syllable sharp with surprise and sorrow. "Ah, William," he said, his voice heavy with feeling. "My old friend."

He knelt and stretched out his gloved hand, holding it before him like a man reaching into a shelf and afraid of what he might find. Then he lowered his hand, all the way to the king's chest.

Walter spoke the king's name again and slapped his face lightly, like a man joking with a friend. He slapped it harder.

Walter stood.

His recent movements had been rapt but unhurried, and not for the first time Simon realized that he did not know this foreign visitor well. He could not decide whether Walter's tense quiet was the result of a temperament suited to danger, or the struggle of a man of uneven intelligence to understand the trouble about to fall on him from all sides.

The marshal would be here in a moment, alerted by the extraordinary silence. Simon stood, too, and folded his arms, feeling very cold. He tried to sort through the events of the last minute, wondering how he could unknot the day, untangle it to find the king alive again, drinking from his skin of wine.

Leaves rustled, the tawny carpet of long-dead oak chaff on the forest floor disturbed by a pair of boots. Roland made his way around the holly tree, his lips already parted as if to ask what was wrong.

He stopped short. Simon could nearly feel compassion at the horror that lit Roland's eyes, and at the sudden anointment of perspiration that gave the marshal's features an inner light.

The marshal's short sword was already in his hand, and he hooked one arm around his hip, like a man who had been stabbed from behind. He was not hurt. He plucked at a sheath, and his fist came out with a long, thin-bladed dirk. He held two weapons.

Walter reached under his cloak and drew a blade of his own. Walter and Simon backed away from the king, and the marshal remained silent as he made his way toward the stricken monarch, a blade in each hand.

The question was all but spoken: *What happened?*

And the answer was as clear in the silent air. An accident. *The* accident, the one all hunters fear.

What the marshal did next mattered very much to Simon. It was as though Roland's touch would have healing powers, and his voice the ability to stop the hour in its course.

Roland knelt, setting aside his short sword, the blade flat

on the chips and fragments of leaves. He felt for a pulse in the king's neck, closing his eyes, looking nearly overcome by shock or grief or more—some harm to his own spirit increasingly sapping his powers. Or perhaps he was offering a prayer, thought Simon, the most heartfelt a royal guardsman would ever offer.

This is my last hour, Simon thought. *The weapons of the king's men will hurt when they cut into me, axes and swords severing limbs, cracking bone. It will not be a quick end, either.* He had seen the hounds seizing the weasel, the wiry, cunning carnivore torn and torn again, its limbs struggling, its jaws snapping even when they no longer lived.

He would die with a prayer on his lips.

But not quite yet. Simon was not ready to join the king in death right that very moment.

Like a beggar silently pleading the necessity of mercy, Simon advanced on the marshal, one hand out. Roland picked up the short sword and rose. He retreated from the dead body, and was calling out, "Hoi! hoi!"—a cry of alarm that could be mistaken as a call for the huntsmen to start after the startled deer.

Except that the marshal's voice was rasping and nearly soundless, some alteration in his sense of purpose impeding him. But he took a breath, to cry out again, and this time the determination was clear.

The marshal's call was powered by a lungful of air—

"Hoi!"—a long note, the one that ordered *Look here*, but also meant *Get ready*. To a hunter it could only indicate that the game was afoot, while to someone already awakened to a felony it meant that trouble was far advanced.

Every past slight returned to Simon's awareness, every assaulted goose girl, every prick of the sword. Edric's flight, and the enduring poverty of Edric's family, they all sprang to life. The neglect his mother had known, his own instantly dashed hopes, they were all there in the bones and sinews of this gathering fist, and it never occurred to Simon that he could do anything but this.

He struck the marshal with his fist. It was not a light punch, a fending-off, or a blow easily explained as purely a gesture of self-defense. This was a solid, through-put strike, a straight-armed clout with all Simon's weight. The marshal did not fall so much as collapse. He struck the ground like a man who would never rise again.

Until that instant, in one region of his consciousness Simon had felt a lingering hope that events could be combed out, reality made simple and harmless once again.

Some small, sputtering query had wondered if matters could be as bad as they looked. He wanted to find this all a clumsy, hideous joke, the royal taste for comedy extended to brutal lengths. How they would all laugh when the king sat up and pointed comically at Simon, a robust, lively chortle distorting his now ashen features.

The sharp pain in the knuckles of Simon's right hand was evidence, however, of a specific quality in the turn of events. Blood started at the marshal's nose, and his eyes were closed. Except for the arbitrary angles of the marshal's arms and legs, he looked like a man who had been lying there for hours, an effigy waiting for a sculptor to arrange his repose. A thought scuttled out of the dim regions of Simon's resolve.

The definite possibility now existed that the royal marshal was now also mortally hurt. By me, thought Simon. *I have joined the ranks of rebels and traitorous felons. I will not live long.*

Someone approached on tiptoe.

Vexin of Tours took in the sight of the fallen marshal with little interest, but he gazed upon the king with unmistakable disbelief, ripening at once to horror. His nearly paralyzed gaze shifted in small, halting phases from Simon to Walter, and back again to the king's sprawling form. In his great dismay, the famous lover did not look the picture of virile beauty. His artificially colored eyebrows were imprinted on a face that was waxy with shock.

There could be no greater affront to good name or vanity than to be tangled in an incident of royal manslaughter. But Simon hoped that this worldly nobleman would utter some reassurance or offer Walter and Simon some promise of companionship. Even more, perhaps Vexin would be blessed with insight into physiology or the powers of Heaven, and be able to detect some lingering life in the stricken monarch.

Vexin spun on his heel and ran.

Walter put his arm around Simon, like a friend protective of a drunken companion. Simon could feel the frantic pulse within the mantle, belying Walter's outward calm.

He whispered, in a voice barely able to make itself heard, "Simon, we must depart."

· 24 ·

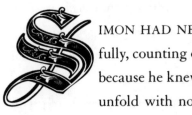IMON HAD NEVER WALKED SO PURPOSE-
fully, counting out the steps—*fifteen, sixteen*—
because he knew that with care the day would
unfold with no further danger. But his steps
had never made such an annoying, troubling *crisp-crisp* across
the many generations of fallen leaves.

Surely, he thought, the huntsmen will call out.

Of course the servants will see the crumpled, heaving form
of the marshal beside the increasingly wax-pale doll, the tangle
of leaf-green clothing, the stubbornly lifeless monarch. The
silence will be lifted, and the day break wide.

But protected by the complicit, almost sentient holly tree,
the gasping marshal and his lord were unseen by the company.
And this secretive, all but silent pace, with the very ravens that

would soon descend, hungry for the dead man's eyes, made Simon feel the profoundest guilt.

Who are you, insisted a metallic inner whisper, *to follow this murderous nobleman while the king lies there like a bloody banquet for the ants?*

Call out, insisted this nagging voice. *Alert the still-unaware company scattered through the woods. You are no better than Walter, if you do not sound the alarm.*

But this shrill consideration was followed by quite a different sort of thought. Was it too late, he wondered, to distance his destiny from that of Walter Tirel?

Walter loosed the killing shaft, Simon would declaim. *I am innocent, a wraith, a vapor, without will or power to choose.*

But some bright-eyed retainer would retort, "Who was it, then, who struck the royal marshal, Simon?"

Had the woods always been this dazzling tangle of green-filtered sunlight and deep, night-flavored shade? Had the ravens always croaked in that incessant, single-note vocabulary, that surely must convey the message *dead-dead-dead* even as it sounded like laughter?

The remaining hunters were stirring. The dog handlers and the riders of the follow-horses restrained their animals, their day still ready, still beginning. They had drawn up at the sight of the stag's escape. They milled quietly now, waiting for the king to give chase. Simon envied them. For them, the king still lived.

Oin the head huntsman no doubt believed that the best part of the hunt was about to begin. He called, "Blood spoor!" alerting the handlers that the dogs best at following a wounded quarry should be loosed from the tethers. He had mistaken the marshal's shout for word that the deer was hurt.

Walter said nothing more, his mantle swinging behind him. Simon followed his example in refraining from speech, and this was further proof that the stiff, frozen spell of the day's events could be broken.

The servants and man-at-arms behind the leaf screen ahead had no inkling what had happened. Walter walked toward them, quickly but with no sign of panic, looking, as he raised a gloved hand, like a man who had forgotten some important implement. Walter had never so impressed Simon as he did now.

Certig offered Simon a questioning look, but said nothing. Even so, something about Simon's glance must have communicated trouble to the veteran servant, who lifted his fingers to his lips as though to silence himself.

Bertram held the bridle of a horse, and he cocked his ear, taking in his master's whispered message.

The man-at-arms gave a nod, as though the tidings were the sort he heard every day, and the knight turned to Nicolas. The expression on his face was expectant, his cheeks flushed.

Simon drew near, expecting to have to steady the herald when he heard the news. But despite his shock he was curious, too, how a knight conveyed such tidings. It was considered bad luck to share bad news without invoking a saint, or without asking for Heaven's help. And it was considered cruel to break the worst sort of news without first giving a word of caution regarding the message.

Besides, Simon tried to believe, unless the event could be translated into speech, perhaps it had not yet really taken place.

"The king is down," said Bertram in a low voice.

Not *The king is slain*. But while not conveying the definitive word, or an even more pungent *The king is dead*, the news could not be mistaken. A quarry that was down, an ox roped in for the slaughter, a tree long accustomed to storm, all could be down for one reason alone. And the very slight softening of the tidings made them all the heavier when the mind briefly weighed and understood.

Nicolas's eyes grew round, but his face took on a look of knowing uninterest, as though the knight was recounting a piece of typical gossip.

Simon wanted to protest. It might not be true. Or it may have been true briefly, but perhaps now the king was choking, gagging, coughing out some new breath and living again.

Someone should go back and look.

The knight added, "We must save Simon Foldre from harm. He is one of us now, and it would shame us if our hunting companion fell into the wrong hands."

Nicolas gave a nod, and all the retainers looking on expectantly would have seen only a young herald and a man-at-arms discussing plans of no interest, and they beheld Walter leaping onto the nearest mount.

Bertram's message made no immediate sense to Simon, even as he climbed into a saddle himself, letting the man-at-arms choose the mount and shoulder him up and into a saddle with a low cantle and a modest pommel, yellow leather and decorated around the margin with crosses, as though to keep the rider in the embrace of Heaven.

The animals waiting here were the most placid of all horses, soft-mouthed mares and experienced geldings, horses who would accept the tumult of the hunt, the sight of frenzied hounds, and the eager cries of huntsmen, without growing excited themselves. These creatures had been intended as decoys, a small, placid herd to make the approaching deer feel welcome.

Simon regretted this pacific quality now as he tried to tickle more speed out of his surprised mare, a moon-gray mount with dark forelegs. The horse cocked her ears at the sound of his unfamiliar urging even as she broke from a willing canter to an all-out gallop.

ARES WERE SOMETIMES POSSESSED OF A quality that folk called simply *marespirit* or *mareishness*.

Simon knew this to be the female counterpart to a stallion's keenness, a willingness to outrun anything and even fight if the need arose. Something in Simon's touch awoke this quality in his long-legged mount, and she flew through the oaks and out into the tussocks and hedgerows, scattering field birds as she coursed.

Simon crouched low in the saddle, grateful for this pale mare's eagerness at leaping the bramble hedges she encountered. Simon had begun by intending to escape the king's men, but now he realized that he might need to escape Walter himself.

The logic was sound. Why should the nobleman suffer the sole witness to survive? With Simon's head severed from his shoulders, Walter could claim that Simon had loosed the deadly arrow—or even that Simon had acted deliberately, out of English malice.

As fleet as Simon's own mare was, Walter must have chosen an even faster horse. When Simon looked back, he could see the nobleman steadily gaining on him. Simon blamed his own bad judgment for wanting this day to be a boy's dream of high excitement. And he cursed his own nature, for trusting his fate to the character of a foreign-born man he did not really know.

Simon tried to run his horse as the hare flees, angling off course only to switch back in the opposite direction, the mare taking heart at this new sport. This gambit was effective at first, but then Walter ran his horse like a greyhound, cutting off the field, and cutting off yet more of the grassland, as Simon ran out of freedom, the corner of the acreage boxed in by a pinfold, a high-walled stone pen for livestock, splashed with lichen and moss.

Simon turned to face his pursuer, his mount lifting her head and ripping at the mossy floor of the pinfold with her dark forehoof.

She wanted a fight, and Simon could only wonder how he could survive even the first attack by Walter Tirel. He was unarmed, or poorly equipped—but surely this knife at his belt would provide him honor as he drew as much blood as he could before he died.

Bertram and Nicolas were approaching, their horses awakened to their task, and far in the rear was Certig, his mount laboring, not wanting to be left behind by the sudden game of trapping Simon in the cold, moss-plastered corner of the livestock pen.

"Where," cried Walter, "are you going?"

"Leave me," said Simon. "Please, leave me here."

It was an impulsive plea, and he knew it would not work. Walter would need to destroy the only witness. But Simon added, "There's a ship nearby, the *Saint Bride*, and the tide is just turning."

Walter said, "Simon, I cannot abandon you here." His voice was ragged, his breath unsteady. While Walter had shown masterly self-control immediately after the event, the swift flight and his growing insight into his predicament had apparently begun to alter his reserve.

Bertram had arrived, his own horse, a strongly built bay gelding, wanting to nose his way into the heavily breathing, spirited assembly.

The knight tossed his head, indicating the east, and said, with an effort at calm, "We must hurry to the river." Bertram added, "My lord, I believe your friend Lord Simon fears you more than the king's men."

Simon had seen before that Walter took his time in recognizing the turnabouts of communication. Only now did the nobleman realize what fear forced Simon as far into the live-stock pen as he could go, sawing at the reins and backing the mare into the deepest shadows.

Walter lifted his sword hand. His glove was stained with water splashed up from the field, and there was blood, a line of uneven staining along the palm. Within the leather his fingers were trembling.

This sign of deep feeling on Walter's part shook Simon. It showed that the nobleman's manner, his well-balanced aplomb, was just that—a manner, a way of behaving. Walter's outward calm did not mean that all was well, or that what had happened could be undone.

"Simon," said Walter, "my friend, you are my companion. If I leave you here, they will hack you to bits."

Nicolas, the herald, had arrived by then. His own horse nuzzled Simon's mare excitedly, nose to nose. Nicolas took a steady look at his master and another at Simon.

"My lord," said Nicolas, adopting formal language, "gives you to know, Lord Simon, that he is a man of chivalry and that he will defend you with his life."

His phrasing was perfect. But the lad spoke with a voice barely under control, a blanched copy of his usual poise.

Bertram, too, who this morning had been the picture of solid attendance, seized the bridle of his master's horse, and gestured pleadingly, *Away, away*.

"I give you my word," said Walter, "that you are safe with me."

This reassurance was exactly what Simon had needed to hear, but he was aware that Walter, for all his quality, was a man of dynamic and changeable temper.

"I'll see that you escape with your lives," Simon said simply.

"My gratitude," said Walter, "will be undying."

At that moment Certig's mount cantered into the shadow of the pinfold, the old servant asking, "What's wrong, my lord Simon? Tell me what has happened." But Certig knew already, or had guessed, tears in his eyes.

The rugged Certig of earlier years would have been the steadiest of all. But since his injury Certig had been easily confused, and now when the old servant wanted to disbelieve what had happened, searching for any reason to think all would be well, Simon did not have the heart to tell him.

A horn was sounding a distant piercing note, followed by a sour high note, the brassy message *Come all, come all* softened and filtered by its passage through the woodland and the humid afternoon.

Simon thought he understood why. In the confusion after an accident, Simon had heard, hunters often looked to themselves, fleeing the scene—especially when an active, deadly swordsman like Roland was present to enact instant vengeance.

Unless, of course, the marshal was still stricken. Additional horns were sounding in the woods. One was the silver-chased ox horn of the royal hunt, but another joined in from a far-off place, its shrill sound muffled by the distance, a series of notes. Another horn responded from the horizon.

Horses approached, heavy mounts, and men called to each other. Spear shafts spanked flanks of horses, urging them to greater speed, and when the *menee* sounded next it was close, not far from the high, moss-bound walls of the pinfold.

"Certig," said Simon, in his firmest voice. Simon forced out the words like a man used to giving fighting orders. "Ride to Aldham Manor. Tell my mother to move at once into the tower."

"The tower, my lord Simon?"

"My father's keep," said Simon in a tone of gentle exasperation. "On the hill behind the house. She and Alcuin and the house servants could hold off an army from there."

Certig groaned. "Oh, we don't have to hide there, do we, my lord? What has happened to make us so afraid?"

"The king is dead," said Simon.

"Did our lord king hurt himself?" asked Certig, sounding like child in need of comfort.

Simon let his horse step gently sideways, into Certig's mount, jostling the servant and causing him to gather the reins more firmly in his grasp. This soft collision had its intended result, stirring Certig back into his wits. He said, "I begin to understand."

"We'll hasten down to the river, Certig," said Simon, "and sail the *Saint Bride* to sea."

"By Jesus, you'd better be quick," said Certig. "Hide in Normandy, my lord. They'll never lay hands on you there." Now that he was in possession of his spirits, the old Certig was back in full. "Oh, never fear, Lord Simon—your mother will be secure."

Before Simon could say more, heavy horses arrived, wild-eyed and dancing as their riders pulled them back. Walter and his companions were trapped in the livestock fold by five of the marshal's men, resplendent in their blue-and-gold surcoats—with Grestain in the lead, a broadsword in his hand.

· 26 ·

SIMON REALIZED THAT ACTUAL FIGHTING would not be much like the pretty, long-winded ballads, in which a wounded adversary swooned and woke and offered up a prayer in rhyme, forgiving the victor. And yet he was not prepared for what actually happened.

"Stand aside, before Heaven," cried Nicolas, in a piercing voice amazing from such a slight youth, "for the passage of Lord Walter, lord of Poix and peer to the crown of England."

This command was given in such a ringing, disciplined manner that three or four of the horsemen drew all the harder on their reins. Their horses backed, snorting, shaking their bridles.

But Grestain, the royal sergeant, stood in his stirrups, as

though Nicolas had not made a sound. This Grestain—so fond of his days herding oxen, thought Simon—is the mortal who will deliver me to death.

It was clear that Bertram and his companions were not equipped for fighting. Simon had a knife at his belt, but nothing else, and even Walter, aside from his bow, carried only a shortsword, a modest weapon compared with a war blade. Bertram was likewise outfitted for the hunt, with a short sword in a brass-chased leather scabbard, and he wore no helmet or body armor.

Grestain, by contrast, was a royal sergeant and accustomed to arming himself with little warning. His leather helmet gleamed, the nasal guard that extended before his face making him look cross-eyed with determination. The other riders and their heavy stallions were likewise armed for combat, with only a few dangling buckles betraying their haste.

Bertram urged his mare forward with a gentle click of his tongue, like any placid rider. He was tall and broad-shouldered, but looked like a man more prepared for diplomacy than bloodshed.

It began as a feat of horsemanship.

Bertram encouraged his mare to ride into Grestain's war-horse with a gentle but insistent, "Press on, press on."

The mare needed little encouragement.

The stallion responded with a snort, pawing the air with a forehoof, and instantly the mare fought back, taking a nip out of the stallion's ear. Soon the animals were squalling like gigantic cats, the big warhorse towering over the mare, the smaller horse seizing the stallion's neck in her teeth and hanging on.

Grestain, encumbered by shield and sword, could not cling to the reins. He toppled sideways out of the saddle, but after his clumsy, arm-waving effort to keep his balance, the gleaming broadsword was no longer in Grestain's grasp. The weapon had found its way into Bertram's hand, and the knight began cutting great slices out of the increasingly helpless Grestain.

The assembled horsemen crowded forward to defend the sergeant, but Bertram made short work of thrusting and stabbing, using the mare as a battering ram against the larger, less determined mounts. Two saddles were empty, then a third, until only one royal guard remained on horseback, in full retreat back toward the woods.

Simon was aghast at this sudden butchery, but fascinated, too, at the deftness shown by Bertram even now. He backed his increasingly uneasy horse out of the widening pond of flesh and gore, and with an air of a woodchopper ready for his next task, turned to learn his master's will.

Simon was further surprised at Walter's reaction to this violence. He gave no sign of concern for the agony of the men still writhing, facedown in the scarlet mud, and he offered no words of praise to Bertram. Walter's manner was that of a man who had seen such sudden death routinely and did not believe that it warranted comment. The violence calmed Walter, and he looked around with a smile to see if Simon, too, was feeling increasing confidence.

Walter accepted the gift of the broadsword from Bertram, along with its belt and sheath, and buckled the weapon on with a look of worried satisfaction. He hooked his thumb into his belt and swelled in the saddle, as though he had felt quite shabbily dressed until now.

Walter murmured a quiet command to Bertram, and the knight rode off beside Certig, a small herd of sheep parting, scattering, and reforming with resilient meekness as the horsemen passed.

Simon envied the sheep that instant—by the day's end these animals would be cropping this very grass under a lively summer rain shower, kept safe by their very number. He envied Bertram and Certig, too, heading off to the thick stone walls and experienced housemen of Castle Foldre.

There was no such promise, Simon knew, that he would be so much as breathing by day's end. Without Bertram and Certig, Simon felt all the more defenseless.

He knew an ancient path that bisected the pastureland, plunged straight through a field of nettles where Caesar the goat stood with his feet spread, chewing earnestly, tethered to a stake.

The horses were eager, well into the mood of what they took to be the day's sport. Nicolas looked ever more youthful, punished by the sunlight sifting down through the clouds, but he was a skilled horseman, riding flank like an experienced squire.

There was about the afternoon a feeling of reprieve, like that moment when a fragile earthen vessel topples and before it strikes the ground, an impression that perhaps, with a little further luck, jeopardy might prove to be an illusion.

They rode hard.

A SMILE LIT UP GILDA'S FACE AS SIMON AND his companions approached.

She was so beautiful in the afternoon sun, her countenance such a relief from the events Simon had just witnessed, that he was swept with emotion.

"What are the horn blowers telling us?" she asked.

Gilda had been carrying a wicker basket down to the ship, the freighter alive to the tide, the unanchored ship stretching her mooring cables, the ship eager to depart like a living thing made of spruce and tar. Walter made a gracious gesture from horseback as he rode down toward the river, acknowledging her with a show of courtliness, and Nicolas offered her a pleasing, "Good afternoon, my lady."

Gilda's spirits began to wilt.

Simon realized what an enigmatic group they must be, all courtesy and tense smiles, while their horses were spiky with blood and spattered with the claylike mud of the local byway.

Gilda's smile was further replaced by an expression of concern as Simon's companions rode their mounts to the river and out into the water. The horses splashed the current with their muzzles, taking a moment to drink, the water around them stained dark at once with mud and with gore.

Walter climbed aboard the vessel and turned to help Nicolas on board, with the air of a man who owned and disposed of everything within sight—including the services of the astonished Oswulf, standing beside the ship's tiller. Tuda, Oswulf's chief rope mender and seaman, climbed up from the ship's hold, his mouth agape.

Simon told Gilda, "We require the ship."

"What do these people want?" called Oswulf, indicating Walter and his herald as though they were a pair of beggars who had blundered onto the vessel.

Simon repeated his statement to Gilda's brother in a voice that would have been audible across the river.

"The ship is not available for hire," called Oswulf, without explanation or courtesy, ignoring his visitors and preferring to speak at a shout with Simon.

Walter had the manner of so many aristocrats, believing that his station in life, his wealth—and his skill with sword and lance—made speech unnecessary and even a little unseemly.

He would not engage in a parley, and he certainly would not utter a word of English. He folded his arms and waited.

Oswulf, for his part, ignored Walter, making a point of having freight to secure, canvas to tug into place, matching a nobleman's arrogance with a freeman's disdain. Tuda took his master's stance as an unspoken command, and he worked a sweep through an oarlock, getting ready to push the ship off with the long oar.

Nicolas set to work rearranging cargo on the deck, and Tuda smiled, pleased to have a helping hand.

"Oswulf, will you take us to Normandy?" asked Simon, riding to the river's edge and dismounting.

"I won't," said Oswulf, with deliberate bad manners, rubbing his nose with the back of his hand.

"The ship is ours," responded Simon, realizing as he spoke that his rights as a lord of all the farmland around did not extend to piracy. It was true that, in an emergency, a man and his ship could be pressed into service, but free folk like Oswulf and his sister would have to be paid a fair price.

Oswulf moved deliberately, but his actions were emphatic. He sprang from the ship and hurried through the shallows to the stony bank. He seized a mooring peg from the shore, a tall, heavy stake with one sharp end and the other shaped like a mushroom from being struck with hammers and mauls over the years.

He held the object like a club. His message was clear.

This was his ship, this his mooring place. He would do what he chose. "Our ship needs no passengers, Simon. We are full of Aldham cheese for the merchants of Brugge harbor." He lowered his voice. "What is this the horn blowers are saying? What's wrong?"

"Walter will pay a good fee," said Simon.

"Surely, Oswulf," urged Gilda, "we have room for three gentlefolk."

Oswulf said nothing.

"What has happened?" Gilda asked, turning to Simon.

It was easy for Simon to understand Oswulf's position. He was protective of his sister, not wanting her to spend shipboard hours or even days with a high-handed Norman lord. And he felt resentful of Simon's ability to play the English and the Norman lord all at once, and perhaps was even further confused as to Simon's ultimate loyalties.

Simon could see that Oswulf understood that something uncommon had happened, and that a crisis was unfolding. Furthermore, he had a businessman's sense that, as the owners of the sole ship of any substance on this stretch of the river, he and his sister could secure a good, round purse.

"Oswulf, take the price he offers you," said Simon.

"Why?" Oswulf seemed to like the sound of his own obdurate inflection.

He made a show of sauntering past Simon, gazing up toward the trees. It sounded as though horses were approaching, a good many, and coming on fast. "Why should some crisis in the woods have anything to do with my sister and me?"

"He'll take the boat without your leave, otherwise," said Simon.

Lord Walter was still wearing his sweeping hunting mantle, and leaning against the rail, he looked like a gentleman in no hurry and quite pleased at the way Nicolas was stowing the huge, wax-coated wheels of cheese into the hold.

"He certainly will not take the ship," said Oswulf in a confrontational tone, awakening to a new stubbornness.

"Accept his silver, Oswulf," Simon pleaded, but the big Englishman brushed past him, hurrying down toward the vessel that gave every sign of being ready to depart in his absence.

Perhaps Oswulf realized the tactical error he had made, leaving the two strangers with only Tuda to attend them. Nicolas was already hauling on the severed length of mooring cable, and the ship was turning with the outgoing tide, her prow quick to catch the current toward the sea. Far from hindering this effort, Tuda was working hard with the oar, compelling the keel away from the shore.

Oswulf hurried, climbing over the side. He seized the tiller of the broad freighter, just as the vessel began to make way toward a half-submerged stump. At the same time a new sound reached them, the high notes of an alarm, and another one across the woodland, two ascending notes, echoing along the river. The horsemen had arrived, and were taking positions along the bank beyond the trees.

Simon accepted Walter's help in climbing on board the ship, and in turn assisted Gilda. The vessel was already slipping well into the current, the rocky bank drifting away as the abandoned horses accepted their freedom, plunging playfully like dogs in the water.

"Master of the ship," said Nicolas, using the English title of respect, "my lord gives his word of honor, before all that is holy, that you and your vessel will be rewarded."

Oswulf shook his head with a confused frown, acting out the role of a river man confronted with the incomprehensible. But when he spoke he was less blunt, showing that he had understood enough. There was a shift in his tone—even a stubbornly single-minded river merchant like Oswulf realized that months and years later he would see Simon in church and at market, and that intractable behavior was unwise as well as unneighborly.

"Simon, do tell me, please," he said, softening his manner. "Why should we endanger our lives and our ship?"

Simon could not for a long moment bring himself to broach the tidings.

"Something terrible has happened," he allowed himself to say.

Oswulf's eyes were round with the unspoken question.

Simon made a gesture, the wave of his hand that meant that he could bring himself to speak no more.

"What is it?" asked Oswulf.

Riders rode hard up and along the bank above. Commands were barked, horses snorting, spear shafts clattering against stirrups as Simon got ready for a hail of arrows, or the whistling approach of a javelin.

Simon said, "The king has been killed."

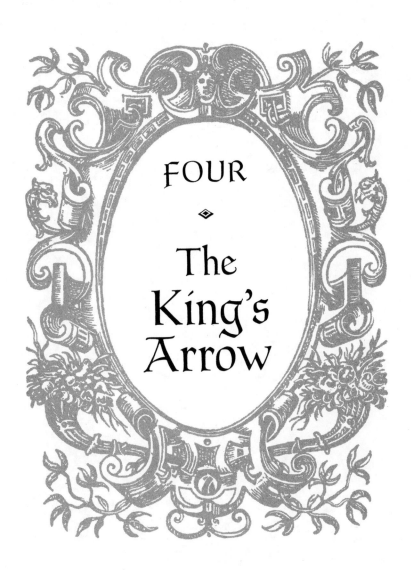

FOUR

❖

The
King's
Arrow

· 28 ·

ROLAND MONTFORT SPOKE, BUT WITH every word blood bubbled from his lips.

He could stand, and he could execute a halting step, but he felt lost to his normal powers. Roland stretched out a hand, and the oak tree beside him offered support. Undersergeants scurried around leading horses, the huntsmen scattered by now, everyone not absolutely bound by duty running off. The incident was too great, and no one would want to admit that he had witnessed the king's dead body.

Roland was glad he was in pain, because with the king dead it was honorable and even necessary to suffer. It was a way of mourning, and a way of experiencing a wrathful humor. His very flesh was heated, and when he gave a command, telling

Grestain to ride out and lay hands on the killer, the words made a bone in his skull vibrate and caused his vision to blur.

"But don't slay Lord Walter," Roland instructed his sergeant in conclusion, blotting his mouth on his sleeve. "Bind him well, and bring him back alive."

Roland called for Oin, the chief huntsman. "Let no one else escape the woods," he said.

"The men of good name have ridden off already, my lord marshal," said Oin. The huntsman wiped his tears. In his sorrow, he was waiting for some further instructions. He was a bluff, agreeable man who could calm dogs and servants with a nod. Oin could run a stoat to ground, but he would be useless, Roland knew, in a fight against other men.

The sergeant's man returned shortly and said that the knight Bertram de Lis had killed Grestain. He gasped out his news before Roland could question him, a ragged recitation that sounded shameless, as though Walter and his cohort were an act of God that no guardsman could confront and survive. The marshal was tightening the saddle girth of a big stallion as he heard the report of his sergeant's death.

He was silenced by an instant of sorrow. Then he asked, "How did the good sergeant die—by sword, ax, or spear?"

"My lord," came the undersergeant's answer, "by the might of his own blade, taken from him by Bertram."

Those full-blooded Norman knights could fight, thought Roland. You could hold off an army with three men like Bertram. The undersergeant addressing Roland now was

Aubri, with a cowherd's accent and a youth's flushed cheek. Roland had thought Aubri had ridden north, toward Winchester with the prince.

But it was like scolding a duck, chiding a youth like Aubri. Roland kept his mouth shut. He felt flush with purpose, grim and wrathful. Roland had possessed one task in life, his single reason for eating and sleeping the king's safety, and Walter Tirel had drawn a bowstring and destroyed it all.

Many riders gathered now, recent arrivals from the lodge wanting to avenge the king, and to avenge their fallen sergeant, too. They were an agitated lot, still strapping on their helmets and buckling on their swords, but Roland would whip them into a fighting force in an instant.

There was no mystery what Walter was going to attempt. His ancestral home of Poix beckoned as a haven, and Roland gave the instructions clearly, each syllable causing the little fissure in his skull to vibrate painfully. Any pursuit would require ships.

"My lord, wait one moment, if you please," said a familiar voice.

It was none other than Climenze, the undermarshal.

"I thought you were with the prince," exclaimed Roland in surprise. "In Winchester, on your way with him to London— along with Aubri."

"My lord, I was directed here," said Climenze. "By the prince himself."

"By Heaven's mercy, you can help," said Roland, pleased

to see Climenze after his initial surprise, and setting aside any puzzlement.

"My lord Roland," the undermarshal was saying, "if you would consider what proceedings would please our royal prince."

Roland marveled that this son of a mule driver could have learned to speak like a clerk. It was the surest way to advance in the world of circumspect and violent men—speak like one of them.

"Prince Henry," said Roland, irritated that any explanation was required, "will surely want Walter manacled and set behind walls."

"My lord, the king's death—" began Climenze. The words stopped him. Climenze made a visible effort and continued, "The king's mishap was purest accident, I warrant, and nothing more."

Roland knew better. A guardsman helped Roland into the saddle. The marshal's ears were ringing. Who would have expected that upstart Simon Foldre to have such a potent right fist?

"Think carefully, my lord marshal," said Climenze, seizing Roland's horse by the bridle, "what the prince and his supporters might have in mind."

Roland raised his voice, even though the effort made a fissure in his skull ignite like red lightning. "Our duty!" he cried.

"Our duty to the king," came the breathless, eager cheer from the horsemen all around. But perhaps they were not so fervent as he might wish, Roland thought. Perhaps the spirit of the men would kindle only when they spied their quarry. No doubt they were bemused with unexpected grief over the fallen king, and would take time to rise to the pursuit.

The royal marshal rode hard, scattering geese, flushing a billy goat, bramble hedges and puddles all but vague impressions.

Climenze rode along with the rest. No one wanted to be left out of this fierce chase. The lord marshal knew that a new song would ring throughout the kingdom after this day—the story of Walter of Poix seized, Walter brought to London in shackles, Walter confessing for the good of his soul.

And Simon Foldre, thought Roland. Yes, that half-Norman upstart—he would beg for mercy, too.

· 29 ·

IMON REALIZED AS SOON AS HE HAD delivered the news of the king's end that his choice of words, and the truth they conveyed, could have been more artfully expressed.

Gilda put a hand out to the side of the ship to steady herself at the report, seizing one of the sail sheets and causing the furled canvas to creak and sway, the entire mast describing a tight circle in the sky. Oswulf reeled, too, deck pegs squeaking all the way to the prow.

When he could manage to make a further sound, Oswulf said, "Simon, get them off my ship."

An arrow snapped through the air, missing the ship and splashing in the current beyond. The passage of the humming projectile and its entrance into the water was much like the flight of a swift or a barn swallow, quick-flying birds that never meant any harm to human beings.

The contrast between the happy hum of the arrow and the instant death that it implied made Simon feel all the more concerned at the predicament he had forced upon his companions. He felt responsible for encouraging Walter to go hunting and had a dismal insight into events. He realized that without his own discovery of the antler in the woods—it seemed ages ago now—the king would still be alive.

Walter gave the riverbank a thoughtful, calculating glance. It was possible to dodge an approaching arrow, with nimbleness and luck, but not if several arrows arrived at the same time.

"Simon," said Oswulf, not belligerent now so much as pleading, "I don't want this trouble."

As he spoke he made an effort to steer the ship away from the bank, across the widening circles the vanished arrow had made in the water as Nicolas, unbidden, began working at the ropes binding the sail.

Borne almost entirely by the outgoing tide, the ship was at first slow to answer the tiller, but as the weathered canvas fell open, the keel made a satisfying sound beneath their feet, and the entire ship's frame shivered with gathering speed.

Another arrow, its white feathers flashing, sang through the air. There was no arc to its flight, the arrow describing a long, straight line across the ship and far off, toward the distant opposite embankment. Archers were testing the range, and at the same time they were letting the ship's passengers know that they would make easy targets.

To preserve his own life and the life of his sister, and to save the ship from the harm an iron-tipped arrow could do, Oswulf levered the ship further into the main current. The sail bellied steadily with the wind, and Simon began to feel the first real hope.

"Our price is ten shillings a day," said Gilda, "for my brother's service, and ten for mine, and another ten for the use of the ship." She was pale, one hand on the ship's rail to steady herself. Simon had to admire her pluck.

But there was no reason for Gilda and her brother to panic. The two arrows had shown that the archers were capable of killing them, choosing their shots. But they also demonstrated that Walter's illustrious name, and the uncertain justice of killing river folk whose vessel had apparently been commandeered, made the bowmen cautious.

"Your price is too high," protested Simon.

No one living near New Forest avoided hard bargaining, and many people enjoyed it. Simon was not one of them.

"What, Simon," asked Gilda, "are his lordship's choices?"

Gilda's offer was far from cheap. The service of an experienced man-at-arms could be had for five shillings a day, and many freemen accepted payment in blocks of salt or candle wax, or even ells of wool, and considered themselves to be on the road to prosperity.

"And his lordship," added Oswulf, "agrees to pay for as much of the cargo as salt water might ruin. And he'll pay us a further ten shillings per day for our trip home."

This could run to a considerable expense. A voyage across the Channel could take anywhere from overnight to a month, depending on weather and currents, and an easy voyage out was often followed by a rough passage back. The *Saint Bride* might prove to be a ruinously expensive vessel.

Gilda gave her brother an appreciative smile, and then she looked at Simon and lifted one eyebrow expectantly.

"And," she said, "we'll see his silver now."

Simon could not believe what he was hearing. "Now?"

"Simon," said Gilda with a show of patience, like someone explaining the obvious to a child, "we need to have a grand deposit on the voyage, or this man of illustrious name might well disembark once we reach the safety of Normandy and leave us without so much as a farthing."

Walter acted the part of the nobleman trusting that his companions would arrange all the details, but his gaze continued to search the trees above the river. He shot a questioning glance at Simon, and Simon in return made a gesture of reassurance he could not at the moment feel.

He was quietly furious with Gilda and her brother, and astonished that they could treat an old friend with so little heart. At the same time, Simon realized that Gilda was no doubt playing for time, believing that as long as she and her brother delayed, quibbling over money, the royal guard would have time to crowd the bank with bowmen, and boats, fast and many, could be summoned to block the mouth of the river.

But Simon felt that he knew Walter Tirel's character fairly well by now. He recognized that this aloof, handsomely mantled figure could commit unexpectedly violent acts. Simon would feel bitterly responsible if Walter felt he had to draw his sword.

They all heard the next arrow's approach, a wasplike keen impending from the dark trees. Even Walter, for all his practiced self-possession, ducked his head reflexively at the sound. But there was no following report of impact, and no further evidence of an arrow—no splash, and no lancing flight toward the opposite bank.

The ship's ropes continued to grow alternately taut and slack as the vessel worked, and the sail was ripe with the wind. No harm, thought Simon.

No harm had come.

There was, however, an additional, delayed gasp of surprise, and an in-taken breath.

And, after a long moment, a body tumbled heavily onto the deck.

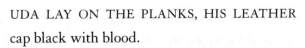

UDA LAY ON THE PLANKS, HIS LEATHER
cap black with blood.

An arrow jutted from his temple, his arms
and legs thrown just as they had fallen, powerless to move. Blood and dark matter from his ruptured horse-
hide cap spilled across the deck as the ship inclined.

Simon fell to his knees.

Oswulf wailed, and Gilda had to take the tiller as her
brother knelt on the deck and made every effort to shake Tuda
back to life.

Simon was shocked beyond words. He knew Tuda's family, with their landmark henhouse. Simon could not bring
himself to imagine the grief Tuda's loss would bring throughout New Forest.

"They killed our Tuda," cried Oswulf.

When Oswulf resumed his place at the tiller, his jaw had a determined set, and there was no talk of turning back, or of the price of the voyage, as the ship rode the swift tide and the rising wind.

"The Devil take you, Simon," said Oswulf after a silence, "and the old king and the new king Henry, or whoever it will be, and all the rest." He spoke in anger, but like someone resigned to whatever further disgrace would take place.

Gilda stood beside her brother in a show of sibling concord, united in their fury and sorrow. Simon understood that to Gilda, her brother was both a responsibility and a source of support, but Simon was disappointed in her. He doubted that he would ever again enjoy Gilda's smile, or take pleasure in her touch—or ever want to.

Walter shrugged off his hunting mantle and spread the soft-woven, forest-green cloth over the crumpled form of the fallen Tuda.

"This is a great pity," said Walter, with a bow toward Gilda and her brother. His gesture was especially gracious, as he crossed his arms over his breast and inclined his head in prayer. His silent entreaty to Heaven complete, Walter said, "I will pay any price you ask."

His statement was not made in English, but it was easy to understand. This was not the first time that Simon had admired Walter's command of the moment, but he marveled that a nobleman of such high feeling could, at the same time, be such a burden. His remark was understood well by Oswulf and Gilda and, stricken though they were, this act of homage evidently touched them.

And the Tirel family was known to have no shortage of silver. Oswulf ran his hand through his hair, perhaps calculating what their voyage might bring.

Gilda said, in a tone of devotion quite unlike her recent, smart speech, "Lord Walter, God help us all."

Another arrow hummed across the ship, but two or three subsequent projectiles splashed wide to the stern, the archers beginning to lose the range. The skills of the bowmen no longer mattered, Simon knew. Somewhere ahead, along the water-way's broad mouth, in ships they had pressed into service, the royal guard would attempt to capture the *Saint Bride.*

Simon squinted into the salt spray. He associated the sea with shipwreck and storm. On horseback Simon felt he could equal the efforts of the royal guard, and he was not afraid to fight with his feet planted firmly on pastureland—especially with Walter battling at his side.

But Simon did not see how they could survive a sea skir-mish. Prince Henry would surely be the next king of En-gland—Simon was sorry that he would not survive to see the new king take on his responsibilities, and to learn what improvements, if any, he might make over his late brother's reign.

Both the immediate future, and the following years to come, would remain unknowable. He and his shipmates, Simon believed, would be dead too soon to afford them any experience beyond the taste of this salt wind and the sight of the approaching seaway.

But the *Saint Bride* showed spirit.

Buoyed, no doubt, by the promise of reward, Oswulf did not give evidence of any further second thoughts. He let the big freighter bank harder, until the side of the ship cut through the water and her passengers had to cling to keep from falling overboard.

The marshal's forces had evidently commandeered three ships, but with summer weather promising pleasant passage for fishermen and merchants alike, most of the speedy vessels were already abroad. The shipyards offered vessels under repair, at such short notice, and two of these were lumbering craft with weathered-darkened sails and tar-clogged rigging.

These ships were slowly making way, and Simon wondered if the dim enthusiasm of the mariners, pressed into emergency service, might be the cause of the halting way the sails were shaken out, the oars slow to stir the water.

Soon only one boat—with a fresh, white sail—breasted the swells in the *Saint Bride*'s wake. She was a swift vessel, with a cunning shape to her prow, and she was on a course to intercept the speeding freighter. But stoical despair had been replaced by the first stirrings of optimism. Simon reasoned that the *Saint Bride* had such a head start, and was so expertly helmed, that no pursuer stood a chance.

But this following craft was amazingly fast in the water, and painted with a long red stripe just below her top rail. She was not a large vessel, and Simon tried to take heart in the fact that in a collision the smaller craft would be at a disadvantage. Several men clung to the rails of this vessel, using their weight to counterbalance the fleet little ship as she heeled, on a course to follow the larger ship.

Or, perhaps, to intercept her. The foam was white at her prow.

"What swift little seacraft is that?" Simon asked wonderingly.

"The *Saint Victor*," said Gilda evenly, "built this past winter from old timber by Mewan and his sons."

Old timber meant that although she was a newly Christened vessel, her wood was not green, and she would not be subject to swelling or leaking. She would be able to maintain her speed.

"Simon, what should we do?" asked Oswulf, for the first time showing deference to Simon's judgment.

"Outsail her, Oswulf," said Simon. "Look, she's hitting our wake."

"She'll cut across our spray," said Oswulf, "and then she'll work back to intercept us."

"She can't be that fast," protested Simon.

Oswulf said, "I sold Mewan the canvas myself, the best Flemish linen. *Fast* does not do her justice."

Simon's hopes began to falter.

"Not," he asked, "Mewan of Docken?"

Oswulf gave a regretful nod. "The very one."

· 31 ·

EWAN OF DOCKEN WAS A FAMOUS SHIP-
wright, whose vessels sailed faster than a
prayer, as the saying went, and the fruits of
whose talents only a royal court could afford.
But the *Saint Bride* had a reputation of her own, and Simon did
not allow himself to despair.

Simon counted four crossbows in the following ship—the
heavily built sort used in sieges and skirmishes, each weapon
bolted and ready. The fast little ship was already little more
than a long bow shot away.

Simon could also make out the unmistakable identity of
the individual leaning forward in the prow. Marshal Roland
kept his balance with care, a lance in his grasp, as he turned
to give commands to the man at the tiller, one of the men

nearby rising to adjust the crisp, new sail. Simon was glad to see the marshal alive, and yet the sight gave him only unsettled relief.

The marshal called something into the wind, his voice warped by the breeze, enjoining the *Saint Bride* to halt or escape any hope of mercy. It was hard to make out his words.

Roland's face was swollen, the sight of his nose caked with blood even now giving Simon's fist a memorial twinge. Climenze, the undermarshal, put out a hand to steady the marshal.

Roland used the lance as a staff, propping himself up in the bow of the sailing vessel. It was easy to see Roland calculating the distance before he could begin plunging the long, iron point into the fugitives on the *Saint Bride*.

"Lighten the ship," commanded Oswulf.

No one moved, certain that they had misunderstood.

"Go on," said Oswulf, "the burghers of Brugge will have to eat leftover rinds for supper."

Gilda responded by hopping down into the hold and hefting out a wax-gray cartwheel of cheese. Unaided, she tumbled this wheel down the sloping deck, and wrestled it into the water. The cheese plunged below the surface, only to reappear again, bobbing and sinking by turns among the swells.

Nicolas and Simon joined her, and soon even Walter was lending a hand, lightening the ship's load. Their efforts caused the vessel to bound more freely over the choppy water as the river current met the salt expanse, and the wind grew fresh.

Wheels of cheese bumped together and slowly spun on the surface in the ship's wake, looking like random stepping stones for an unearthly titan. This waste of valuable freight—and delicious bounty—pained Simon and made him feel all the more responsible for the day's grief.

But for a while this loss of ballast did speed the ship along, and Simon believed that with every heartbeat the white sail of the *Saint Victor* was more remote.

"I told you," exulted Simon. "We'll leave her in our wake."

"She's switching back," said Oswulf, "to cut us off."

She's not, Simon wanted to protest.

Oswulf grimaced into the salt spray. "The *Saint Victor* will play the foxhound, and we'll all see what it's like to have our throats open to the weather."

If Certig were here, thought Simon, the old servant would think of a dozen reasons for optimism—each of them false. Simon hated to let the thought enter his mind, but at last it could not be denied.

Oswulf had been right.

The big freighter, which had seemed so admirably swift before, now wallowed with the swells, the sleek, smaller vessel gaining on her easily as the afternoon began to lose color and the late-day shadows began to define the waves of the open Channel.

Simon felt the first drops of rain and saw what was about

to happen as though this gift of insight fell also from the sky.

Every one of his companions was in danger because of Simon, his logic counseled him. He believed further that only he could perform the act that would halt the actions of a dangerous and powerful man and at the same time allow his shipmates to be held blameless.

"Walter," said Simon, "give me the broadsword."

Walter did not respond, clinging to the side to keep his feet steady.

Simon realized that he had failed to remember an important element of courtesy in his request, and so he asked again. "My lord, if you would please be generous enough to allow me to hold the blade for a moment."

This phrasing both dignified and softened Simon's request, and he held out his hand expectantly.

Preparing to confront Roland was not the only reason to take possession of the broadsword—Simon felt that taking such a deadly weapon away from Walter would help to ensure that he and Oswulf could do business without the nobleman doing something impulsive and fatal.

Walter did not make a move to surrender the weapon. His hand rested on the brass pommel of the sword, and he half closed his eyes, weighing whether protocol or necessity demanded that Simon take the blade.

"My lord is pleased to bear this sword," said Nicolas on his master's behalf, "in your defense, and in furtherance of his own honor."

Nicolas was calm, but Simon had recently learned to see through the apparent unruffled air of his associates. Nicolas would rather Simon drew the aim of every crossbow in the approaching vessel, leaving his master unhurt. It would not be proper, however, to say as much.

Simon was no longer a mere varlet, and no longer a novice at witnessing bloodshed. "As my father's son," said Simon, "honor requires me to defend my companions."

Walter said, with a smile, "Well spoken, Simon."

This was high praise, if brief, but Simon felt that Walter was quick with a compliment because he expected that soon Simon would be beyond the reach of human acclaim. And yet Walter still made no move to yield the sword.

Simon did not expect to survive this encounter that approached, angling in on the sleek, white-sailed vessel. He saw his verse in a poem of the day's events, Roland's lance plunging into Simon's chest, his heart's blood flowing, even as he countered with a thrust of the sword, taking Roland's life. Or, as it might happen, failing. Simon was sick at the thought, and yet he was determined.

Walter drew the weapon.

He hefted it in his yellow-gloved hand, the very hand still stained with royal blood. And perhaps Simon was surprised at what Walter did next. Some corner of Simon had hoped that the nobleman would deny him the weapon, and claim that Walter Tirel alone had the name and dexterity equal to slaying the royal marshal.

Walter held the weapon across to Simon, hilt first, bracing his feet against the motion of the ship. Simon had to laugh inwardly, mocking his own aspirations. He had been hoping the sword would not be given to him, even as he had half hoped it would be. Here it was, the well-balanced blade. It felt good in his hand.

Simon said, "My lord, I thank you."

Even if Simon succeeded in striking down the marshal without injury to himself, the little ship that was drawing so near was bristling with crossbow quarrels, and Simon could recite the verse that recounted his blood joining Tuda's, staining the long, smoothly planed planks.

The rain sifted down.

When the voyage arrived at an abrupt stop, time—which had paced slowly—began to take on momentum again. The *Saint Victor* angled to a halt directly ahead of the freighter, and to avoid a damaging collision Oswulf had to turn the *Saint Bride* across the wind. Gilda adjusted the sail, tying an efficient knot, and both vessels came to in the easy swells.

The two vessels were still a long spear's length apart, but a grappling hook was produced among the marshal's crew, and the long pole with its iron claw was extended across the space.

Nicolas tugged at Simon's sleeve.

"The marshal," advised Nicolas in a low voice, "is wearing body armor under his mantle."

"How do you know that?" marveled Simon. This meant

that the marshal would be proof against a thrust to his body.

"My lord Simon," said Nicolas, his gray eyes blinking against the rain, "last night I slept but little. I spied upon the lord marshal."

"Did you?" asked Simon in a tone of respectful wonder.

Nicolas gave a smile, as much as to say, *I did indeed*.

The grappling pole had found purchase on the side of the *Saint Bride*, the iron talon damaging the wood. The smaller ship closed the gap, fell away as a swell collapsed under it, and then rose up again, nudging the freighter. Other hooks were handed up, binding the two ships together. The big ship's mast rocked, and wooden pegs complained along the length of the keel.

Until that moment Simon and his crew had been free, however straitened their hopes.

Now they were prisoners.

· 32 ·

ROLAND FLUNG ONE LEG OVER THE freighter's rail and climbed on board.

No one in the *Saint Victor* made an effort to help him. He used the lance, point down, to steady his weight, the point making tiny scars in the deck.

He looked bruised and bloodied but as hale as ever, although it appeared to be a challenge for him to keep his balance as the two craft lifted and fell in the water. The remaining royal guardsmen in the vessel looked on with a pensive, neutral air that Simon found curious.

If Roland had shown a combative fierceness and offered an attack with a loud cry and a ringing curse—like the war chiefs in the poems Simon used to love—it would have been much easier to strike at the marshal, and strike again, until he lay motionless.

But what actually happened was less like the poetic histories, and more like a royal protector taking possession of a conveyance and its occupants, all his to lawfully seize. Simon was surprised at Roland's quietly businesslike manner, as though detached from the tumult of the day's proceedings, until he recognized the feeling in the marshal's eyes.

It was grief, Simon guessed, that caused Roland to gaze at Walter, down the length of the big freighter, in such a solemn manner.

"So, Simon," began Roland, with something like weary regard. "You are in league with the slayer of our lord king."

The marshal sounded almost satisfied with Simon's status as a regicide's accomplice, as though this merely confirmed the marshal's long distrust. His lips were swollen, and his voice subdued.

"Lord marshal," said Simon, "allow my friends to escape to Normandy."

The two ships were fast together now. The armed men of the *Saint Victor* remained as they were, Climenze foremost, his crossbow cocked. Roland had no need to hasten his efforts. The entire company of the captured ship could be named traitors and foreign enemies, as the terms applied, and the ship itself be taken as legal plunder.

"Escape?" echoed the marshal, as though the idea was

unthinkable. "I would hunt you and your companions down any hole in Christendom."

"I forced the ship, and her owners," Simon continued, "against their expressed desire and will."

This was, he thought, very nearly the truth.

But Roland was not an officer about to trade a string of declarations with criminals. He made an eloquent gesture, *Away with all of you.*

"Walter Tirel," the royal marshal began, in a ringing voice, "I arrest you—"

For the death of the lord king.

That was what Roland was expected to say, and that was what Simon very nearly heard, finishing the marshal's formality in his mind.

But his utterance was never completed.

· 33 ·

NICOLAS KNELT AT THE MARSHAL'S FEET, looking for an instant like a herald pleading for mercy.

He plucked the opal-handled dagger from the sheath at his hip, and plunged it through the marshal's boot, into his foot, all the way to the wooden deck. The ship shivered perceptibly as the dagger point entered the plank. The marshal's foot was pinned.

Nicolas scrambled away as Roland's lips went white. The marshal fumbled, finding a new grip on his lance. He raised the iron-tipped weapon as Simon closed on him, setting the broadsword harmlessly but forcefully across the marshal's chest, protecting Nicolas.

What happened next shocked Simon even more deeply.

The marshal's head snapped on his spine, and a burst of blood flew from his mouth, splashing Simon's own lips. It was like a calculated insult, a man spitting into another's face. But Simon never mistook the substance, like hot salt on his tongue. At the same time, a barbed iron point, unexplained and beyond any danger Simon had expected, suddenly jutted from the royal marshal's throat as a crossbow bolt struck the marshal from behind.

Roland collapsed as the sword slipped from Simon's grasp.

The marshal made a reflexive effort to pluck at the cross-bow quarrel—surely that was what it was—projecting from his throat, but before he could fold his fingers around the broad iron point, his eyes were fixed, and his hand lifeless. His leg was cocked at an awkward angle, pinned to the deck.

Climenze, the undermarshal, stood in the prow of the smaller ship with the crossbow at his shoulder. As he lowered the now-discharged weapon, he said, with an air of quiet chal-lenge, "Long live King Henry."

The undermarshal looked directly at Simon as he spoke, a squarely built man looking all the larger with having tugged the trigger of his weapon. It was not the first time in recent days that Simon felt that he was being given a test—of judg-ment, and of loyalty.

Climenze had spoken in English: *Long live King Henry.*

As fallen rain cleaned his face of blood, Simon considered how best to respond to a man who had just killed his own immediate superior. It was hard to express routine courtesies, or wish the likely king a long life, with the marshal's blood flowing, barely diluted by the rain.

Walter was at Simon's side, without warning, plucking Roland's fallen lance from the deck.

"What breed of men are you," said the nobleman, "to strike down your master?"

Simon tensed. Walter held the lance as though he had already killed the undermarshal in his mind and was deciding who would be next. The small shipload of men, however, did not look willing to be slaughtered.

Climenze visibly shrank.

"My lord Walter," he said, alarm in his voice, "we beg your mercy."

Walter thrust the spear into the smaller vessel, the iron point taking a bite out of the top rail. The nobleman steadied his feet, still clinging to the lance, and Simon saw what was likely to happen, a different version of the very near future from the one possessed by Walter. Simon could guess too well what a crossbow bolt would feel like, puncturing his own ribs.

He seized the shaft of the lance, and wrestled with Walter, the nobleman's yellow gloves gripping the weapon. Simon knew how unforgivable Walter might find this struggle, and how far beyond any apology or explanation Simon could offer. Walter was strong, and he was more experienced at keeping his footing during bloody strife.

But Simon believed that Walter's mood would alter soon, and that as his temper cooled, the sunset would glow and the soft rain come down warm and forgiving. He hoped Walter's determination would give out immediately—the man used his power like a combatant accustomed to conflict, feinting and recoiling, nearly overcoming Simon.

Simon made one final effort, wrenching the shaft and bringing it down hard, out of the nobleman's grasp. The lance was heavy, and sticky where resin had been rubbed to improve the grip. With the weapon in his hands Simon had an instant of choice, and the power to do whatever he wished—hurl the span away, or run it into Walter's body.

It was not the first time that day Simon knew what it was to have the power to strike fear.

"My lords," cried Nicolas, stepping between them and gesturing to some position well away from the ship. "Look—we are free!"

HE *SAINT VICTOR* WAS BACKING, HER SAIL fluttering, failing to catch, and then bellying with a gentle thunder, taking the wind.

"Farewell, my lords," called Climenze. "And a safe voyage to all of you."

Simon let the lance fall with a clatter.

Gilda picked it up and hung it on a pair of hooks on the side of the ship made for such a weapon. With the lance stowed in a secure place, and the departing vessel reduced to a flap of sail on the shifting swells, Simon felt hope once more.

"Those are creatures of rankest dishonor," said Walter at last, gazing after the already distant ship.

"My lords," Nicolas confided, "we were never in any great danger from the men loyal to Prince Henry."

Walter disputed this with a glance.

"The lord prince, I think," said Nicolas, "plotted his brother's death."

Walter protested, "King William was my good friend." He made a visible effort to force himself to make the admission, audible only to Simon and Nicolas, "It was Marshal Roland that I sought to kill."

"My lord," added Nicolas, "I believe you accidentally killed a king who was going to die today by another hand."

"Nicolas, no brother under Heaven," protested Walter, "would seek his sibling's murder."

Nicolas would not get into a dispute with his master. He knelt and tugged at his knife, freeing it with effort from the marshal's corpse. The marshal's leg had been cocked at an awkward, acute angle, but now it relaxed gracefully, and the marshal looked like a weary and battered man in repose.

The herald's lack of further answer had its intended effect. Walter watched the receding vessel, and glanced around at the open water. He eyed his herald with a quality of friendly suspicion.

"Nicolas," he demanded, "how do you know this?"

Nicolas looked up at Walter and Simon in turn, his face composed and his voice a peaceful sigh as he wiped his knife with a linen cloth.

He said, "I hear much."

"You should have told me," said Walter.

"My lord," said Nicolas, "when do you listen to me?"

The rain, which had been failing, stopped entirely.

They consigned the lord marshal to the sea, with prayers to merciful Heaven for the peace of his soul, and they buried Tuda with him.

The *Saint Bride* sailed all night, and at dawn the Normandy coast showed itself, a line of fields beyond the dunes, dark turning steadily to gold.

FIVE

◆

Chase
End

· 35 ·

HE STALLION'S NAME WAS RASOR—"RAZOR," like a keen steel edge—and he was well named.

He cut the surf with his hooves, racing up over one dune after another. He stood as though to challenge the tossing sea-foam steeds of the Channel, and then galloped away, high-spirited and every bit the appropriate mount for the youthful English lord who, as the recent songs would have it, had helped to save Walter Tirel's life.

Simon liked this horse very much. He liked this Norman seacoast, and its gentle rivers, its cider and its wine, and its people. On a fine day he could gaze across the salt tide and see the loom of green and subtle variation in the sky, the clouds' reflection of the fields and woods of England. He had gotten word that his mother was safe, and Simon felt an urgent need to do nothing—to enjoy the pleasant, peaceful place that had received him so generously.

Nicolas approached on a brisk, quick horse, and called out, "My lord and lady would attend you, Lord Simon."

"I am theirs to command," said Simon, feeling mystified. He leaned from the saddle and asked the herald directly, "Does my cloak need brushing?"

"Can there be anything amiss on such a splendid day?" asked Nicolas, his eye aglow with quiet humor.

Simon persisted, "Has the salt water stained my cap?"

Alena looked down from a safe distance, atop a mount of her own, a soft-mouthed, vivacious mare. Walter was beside her, on a horse that pawed the sand and shook its bridle. Walter Tirel's well-regarded sister was indeed as quiet in temper as people had described. And as beautiful, and she proved less cloistered in prayer than reports had indicated.

Simon dared to have high hopes—the highest sort of aspirations imaginable.

Marriage to such a woman would supply Simon with a generous purse—her dowry would be substantial. But this was not what attracted Simon. He could not put the image of her—or the consideration of her softly spoken speech—out of his mind.

A month had passed since King William fell in New Forest. Word came from England of the new King Henry, crowned the day after his brother's death, in a confident if grief-touched ceremony in Winchester. News came, too, of a pardon and cordial greeting to Walter Tirel and all of his associates. The common understanding was that Henry would be a practical-minded, moderate sovereign, and an improvement over the past.

Nicolas, who knew all the news worth hearing, reported that English and Norman alike were of the belief now that Walter's fatal arrow had been shot by accident, and no further investigation or punishment would be necessary. Nicolas encouraged Simon to think that the new king preferred that version of events—it spared the throne any hint of conspiracy.

The *Saint Bride* had sailed back to England heavy with treasure a fortnight before. With a load of Norman men-at-arms eager to try their luck in the new king's service, paying their way at the highest price, Oswulf and Gilda were happy. But Simon was not eager to return, and his mother had concurred in a message written in Alcuin's neat hand, urging him to try his fortunes among the Normans.

Alena had greeted Simon on his arrival weeks ago with a shyly courteous kiss and an expression of thanks, but Walter's household was largely masculine, as was typical of Norman domestic arrangements, with hearty local dukes and their sons eager to meet this English lord who had helped to rescue their friend.

Being English in Simon's case was not so much a disadvantage as a source of mild wonder. He was very slightly exotic, and half Norman in background after all. The recent mantle of local fame and manly honor was very pleasing to Simon.

In recent days Alena had accepted an invitation to sit with Simon and hear a minstrel sing newly crafted ballads. One of the verses, about the falcon and the squab, was indelicate enough to cause her to lower her eyes and lift a linen kerchief to hide her smile.

On leaving she had touched Simon's hand and said, in a low voice, "Someday, Simon, perhaps there will be a brave song about you."

"Perhaps," Simon had added meaningfully, "about the two of us."

She had smiled.

Now Nicolas was saying, "You appear as you are, Lord Simon, if I may say so—every bit the man of sport and deed."

Nicolas spurred his mount, and joined the brother and sister briefly on the sandy hillcrest. Walter turned to say something to the herald, and then Walter lost no time in joining Simon at the edge of the surf.

Rasor touched noses with Walter's mount.

"My sister," Walter began, "wishes to know you better."

Simon was amazed that his heart could continue beating. "If the lady wishes it, and it pleases you, Walter."

"I believe you have won her attention," said Walter with a quiet laugh.

While consideration of a possible marriage would have

been premature, it was not lost on Simon that as a brother-in-law, he would be bound by allegiance to his wife and her family. In a world that relied on faithfulness to family and good name, Simon would be bound by loyalty to keep the events of New Forest, and Walter's designs on the royal marshal's life, entirely to himself. The events that led to the accidental death of a king would be a secret known by few.

Walter gave his sister a wave, and then urged his mount to an easy trot along the hissing margin of the waves. He continued to ride, his horse indenting a long line of hoofprints to be half erased by the sea.

Alena rode down now to meet Simon, while her brother rode on, far out of earshot. Simon realized that, with her brother's permission, Alena was approaching Simon accompanied by neither herald nor bodyguard. This was no ordinary meeting, framed as it was with formality, and yet providing such an opportunity for shared solitude.

Alena made a soft sound with her tongue and her horse stopped, right beside Simon's. The two horses enjoyed each other's company, nuzzling each other quietly.

"Someday," said Alena, "you will return to England, no doubt."

"I need not go back soon," said Simon.

Alena had been wearing a hood, but she reached up with a gloved hand and pulled the peaked cloth back, so that Simon could see her eyes. For a quiet woman, Simon thought, she had a most direct gaze. Her hair was dark, her eyes green, and when she smiled right at Simon just then, she accidentally lifted the reins, causing her horse to take one pace back.

"Not until you sing me some of your English ballads," she said. "Of the drake and the bread knife, and the hart and the horn," she said, naming two particularly bawdy songs.

"My lady Alena," said Simon, "I know many verses—including those."

"I will let you recite these ballads, Simon, on one condition."

Simon could not speak, he was so tangled in happiness.

"We'll race," she said, with a smile. "If you reach my brother before I do, I am yours to please."

She was off, her cloak swirling behind her, and she was swift in closing the distance between her horse and her brother's distant, cantering mount.

She was already too far ahead.

"Fly, Rasor," urged Simon, and the sand was a blur beneath the hooves. Grit flung up by Alena's mount dashed his lips.

Was it true Alena was turning in her saddle, causing her mare to slow?

Or was Rasor so fleet?